Marian Babson

MURDER ON A MYSTERY TOUR

Walker and Company
New York

MURDER ON A MYSTERY TOUR
Marian Babson

First published in the United States of America
in 1987 by the Walker Publishing Company, Inc.

Published simultaneously in Canada by John Wiley & Sons
Canada, Limited, Rexdale, Ontario.

Library of Congress Cataloging-in-Publication Data

Babson, Marian.
  Murder on a mystery tour.

  Reprint. Originally published: Weekend for murder.
London : Collins, 1985. (The Crime club).
  I. Title.
PS3552.A25W4   1987   813'.54   86-28916

ISBN: 0-8027-5668-9

Printed in the United States of America

10 9 8 7 6 5 4 3 2 1

DEDICATED TO:

Ruth Windfeldt and her
Scene of the Crime Tours

Maggie Brewer and her
I Love A Mystery Tours

Nancy Wynne and Shirley Beaird and their
Murder By The Book Tours

Phyllis Brown and her
Grounds For Murder Tours

Dilys Winn and her
Murder Ink Tours

Chapter House Travel and their
Rendezvous With Murder Tours

Joy Swift and her
Murder Weekends Limited

Charlotte MacLeod—with much thanks for her help

And all aficionados everywhere.

CHAPTER 1

The knives were out at Chortlesby Manor.

Fish knives, butter knives, meat knives, carving knives, bread knives, fruit knives, even—in deference to the visitors expected soon—steak knives, were spread in glittering array across the pantry table.

Below them ranged fish forks, meat forks, salad forks, carving forks, sweet forks, pastry forks and pickle forks. Then came a lower row of soup spoons, sweet spoons, teaspoons, coffee spoons, salt spoons, egg spoons, table-spoons and assorted serving spoons.

The final row was a miscellaneous jumble of sugar tongs, grape scissors, jam-jar lids, salt cellars, cruet sets, knife rests, fish slices, muffineers, nut crackers, nut-meat picks and a dozen fox mask silver stirrup cups.

An all-pervading smell of silver polish hung heavy in the air and the once-pristine butler's apron was grey-streaked and stained. The man wearing it gave a final vigorous rub to a pastry fork and set it down in the proper row. He frowned at it judiciously and picked it up again.

'Oh, let it be, Reggie,' his wife said from the doorway. 'If you get that silver any brighter, they'll have to wear dark glasses at the dinner table.'

'A couple of the last ones did, anyway,' Reggie said, but he replaced the fork and grimaced at his hand. 'Filthy job!'

'I told you to leave it to the help,' Midge said. 'Lettie was mooning around all morning, doing nothing.'

'Steady on, old girl!' Reggie looked at her in alarm. 'Lettie isn't exactly help, you know.' He frowned at her anxiously. 'You *do* remember that, don't you?'

'Oh, I suppose so.' Midge sighed and ran her fingers through her hair. 'It's getting more difficult, though. It never seems to stop. I have to keep closing my eyes and thinking of our mortgage.'

'Hold on to that thought. Life may be more complicated these days, but it means we're climbing out of the red. Besides—' he beamed at her suddenly—it was the old Reggie grin, not the professional Mine Host smile he used so often these days. 'Besides—it's rather fun, isn't it?'

'Rather ... We're certainly getting a different type of guest—not to mention a different sort of complaint.'

'And not even so many of those.' His grin broadened. 'If the service slumps or anything goes wrong, they don't dream of complaining, they just think it goes with the territory.'

The sudden shrill peal of the bell startled them. With a clatter, a black and white card dropped into place in the rows of pigeonholes over the door. Number 22 was at it again.

'Now *there's* someone I'd like to kill,' Midge said. 'I could cheerfully strangle her with my bare hands!' She started for the door.

'Hold on a minute—' Reggie stopped her. 'You don't have to go running upstairs every time she rings. Let's just see what she wants first.' He picked up the telephone, dialled 22 and waited. 'Maybe some day we can even get her to realize that she has a telephone in her room.'

'Not her,' Midge said. 'Having a bell-rope in her room has given her delusions of grandeur. She thinks she's the Lady of the Manor and we're her servants.'

'Yes, Mrs Barbour—' Reggie waved a silencing hand as someone lifted the receiver at the other end of the line. 'Can we help you?'

'Ackroyd is in my room again.' Amaryllis Barbour's carrying voice scarcely needed the assistance of the telephone. 'He refuses to leave. I demand that you come up here and evict him!'

'I don't think that will be necessary, Mrs Barbour,' Reggie said soothingly. 'Just put him on the line and let me have a word with him.'

'Oh, really! Come here and get him—instantly!' The receiver was slammed down violently.

'I'll go up,' Midge said, as Reggie rubbed his ear.

'Ackroyd has a warped sense of humour,' Reggie said. 'He knows that woman hates him. He enjoys upsetting her.'

'Oh no.' Midge paused in the doorway, glaring. 'The *real* reason Ackroyd keeps stalking her is that he knows a big rat when he sees one!'

The thought cheered her all the way up the stairs and twitched the corners of her mouth as she tapped on the door.

'It took you long enough!' Mrs Barbour appeared to believe that someone should materialize the instant she pulled her bell-rope. She stepped back, radiating fury and discontent.

'I'm sorry, Mrs Barbour, we're very busy today.' Midge held on to her temper by visualizing a miniature Amaryllis Barbour clenched between Ackroyd's jaws, arms and legs dangling limply. 'The new guests are due in just a few hours.'

'I hope they're not going to disturb Bramwell,' Mrs Barbour said severely. 'He is communing with his Muse. Nothing must be allowed to disrupt his train of thought.'

The clatter of a typewriter could be heard from the master bedroom opening off the sitting-room of the suite, bearing witness to Mrs Barbour's remarks.

'I'm sure Bramwell will be able to finish his stint for the day in good time to welcome our guests and take part in the festivities.' Midge forced a smile.

'It is not a *stint!*' Amaryllis Barbour bristled. 'Genius knows no boundaries; nor is it ruled by hours. Bramwell does not "stint" his talent!'

Midge took a deep breath and reminded herself that it was nearly over. Just a few more days and she would never have to see either of the Barbours again. She allowed her mind to skip ahead to pleasanter considerations: as soon as they had left, she would disconnect the bell-pull and remove it. No future occupants of this suite would ever be able to demand her dancing attendance again. There were going to be some other changes made, as well. When the new season started . . .

'I'll be glad to see the last of this nonsense.' Unwittingly, Amaryllis echoed Midge's thoughts. 'I simply cannot understand why Bramwell allowed himself to be roped into this charade in the first place.'

'You *have* had a nice holiday, haven't you?' Midge murmured gently. Six weeks in England, with all expenses paid, including free air flights, for only three weekends' work as Master of the Revels was pretty good going in anyone's language.

'Holiday? You call this a holiday? With poor Bramwell working his fingers to the bone?'

A fresh burst of machine-gun typing gave added impetus to her words.

'But I thought Bramwell was delighted that the book was going so well,' Midge said, as innocently as the vitriol dripping from her voice would allow. 'No one's forcing him to work on it. All he has to do is host three weekend parties. That isn't too arduous. Especially as he has Evelina T. Carterslee to act as hostess. She carries half the burden as Mistress of the Revels.'

'And that's another thing,' Amaryllis flared. 'That woman! That *awful* woman! I don't know why you bothered with her.'

'It was all arranged from the States,' Midge said. 'And she *does* have a lot of fans. Most of the guests are delighted to find her here.'

'Bramwell should have been celebrity enough. I could quite easily have acted as his hostess. I always do at home.'

'It wasn't up to me,' Midge weaseled out from under the implied accusation. 'Death on Wheels and The Crimson Shroud organized everything from their end. Chortlesby Manor is just the venue.'

'*Miles* from the nearest town!'

'Only two miles. Some of the guests find it just a pleasant walk. In any case, there's always a car avail—'

'If you call *that* a car! I shall never understand how Bramwell allowed himself to be inveigled into this ridiculous enterprise. He should have had more sense. I don't know what he was thinking of!'

The betting below stairs was that Bramwell had seen it as an opportunity to escape from his mother. Unfortunately, he had underestimated her determination—and her death grip.

Midge made an indeterminate sound and looked around the sitting-room. Ackroyd was crouched beneath the television set, his baleful gaze fixed on Mrs Barbour. Midge wriggled her fingers at him enticingly, but he was not to be coaxed away.

'And another thing—that creature! That Lettie—!'

Midge recognized that they were getting to the nub of Mrs Barbour's complaints now. Ackroyd had simply been an excuse to acquire a listener.

'It's shameless, the way she's always in and out of the bedrooms—'

'Lettie has to go into all the bedrooms every night to turn down the covers. It's part of the routine.'

'That's no excuse. There's no need for her to keep going into Bramwell's. I can take care of that myself.' She sniffed. 'The way that female *flaunts* herself is disgraceful!'

No doubt about it, the old girl had her knife out for Lettie. Probably for any young pretty woman to whom her son was attracted. Not that she needed to worry. Lettie was not fool enough to tie herself up with a mother-in-law like that. Midge wondered how many times Amaryllis Barbour had ruined her son's chances. It could be no coincidence that he was nearing middle-age and still unmarried—not with mother constantly in tow.

'Come on, Ackroyd,' Midge called. There was no point in trying to argue with a brick wall. Amaryllis was Bramwell's problem—and he was welcome to her.

'And that cat should not be allowed to go into the guests' rooms.' Amaryllis was abruptly reminded of her original complaint. 'It's dangerous.'

'Oh, really!' Midge protested.

'It is! He could frighten someone into a heart attack. Or someone could trip over him. Not to mention people who might be allergic to—'

'Come on, Ackroyd.' Midge stooped and scooped him up before he could be blamed for the state of the economy, the attitude of the Common Market Commissioners and the next terrorist attack anywhere in the world. 'You're not wanted here.'

'He certainly isn't! There are too many creatures around this hotel pushing themselves in where they aren't wanted.'

The typing noises beyond the far door had stopped and there seemed to be a listening silence, perhaps even a guilty silence. Neither Lettie nor Ackroyd were unwelcome so far as Bramwell was concerned. Midge couldn't speak about Lettie, but she knew for a fact that there had been definite enticement when it came to Ackroyd: delicious titbits smuggled away from the dining table and lovely pieces of typing paper crumpled into balls for him to chase. It was not surprising that Ackroyd sought the company of this charming playmate.

'I think it particularly distressing that there should be another *invasion* of fans at this time. Bramwell's book is at a crucial stage—' She lowered her voice and spoke with hushed awe. 'Adam MacAdam and Suzie Chong are just about to begin interrogating the suspects.'

Midge cravenly buried her face in Ackroyd's fur to hide her involuntary grimace. She was not a fan of the popular husband-and-wife detective team. Ackroyd took the gesture as no more than his due and broke into a throaty purr.

'So you see, it is imperative that Bramwell not be disturbed at this delicate juncture. He must be free to bring all his resources to bear upon his work.'

The rattle of typing began again in the other room, as

though on cue. Amaryllis Barbour nodded in satisfaction and gave Midge a meaning look.

'You see?'

Midge nodded back without speaking. It was safer that way. Several days ago, Ackroyd had escaped the Barbour suite with one of those crumpled balls of paper still in his mouth. Midge and Reggie had rescued it and smoothed it out to see what sort of prose Bramwell considered beneath his talent. They had discovered a multiplicity of quick brown foxes jumping over lazy dogs. Since then, they had taken a jaundiced view of the rapid-fire typewriter chatter of his supposed creativity. Not that they blamed him. If Sweet Amaryllis had been riding on their backs, they might have stooped to a little honest subterfuge, too.

'I am the mere guardian of a great and noble talent,' Amaryllis Barbour said solemnly, not for the first time. 'It is my humble—yet glorious—destiny in life to stand between my son and those who would use him and toss him aside, those who would plunder his Talent, ravish his Gift—' She drew herself up, her nostrils flared, her eyes flashed fire.

'I will defend him—to the death, if necessary!'

'Er, yes,' Midge said. 'Well, perhaps you'll make his excuses to the company if he isn't able to attend the Opening Reception.'

Amaryllis Barbour took a deep breath and opened her mouth. Before she could launch into another Declaration, Midge, who had been quietly backing towards the door, slipped through it and closed it firmly behind her. She also closed her eyes and took a deep breath of her own.

From the corridor, the frantic typing was mercifully blurred. The loudest sound was Ackroyd's purr. Automatically, Midge ran her fingers through his white ruff and smoothed the long white streak of his chest. The purring grew louder. A rough little tongue dabbed at her fingers.

Midge slumped weakly against the wall, eyes still closed, trying, as she had told Reggie, to think of the mortgage.

Even more cheering was the thought that this was the last weekend the Barbours would be in residence. It had seemed like such a good idea a few months ago, but by now even Death On Wheels and The Crimson Shroud must be having second thoughts. With luck, they would not repeat that experiment.

The sound of a doorknob turning brought her away from the wall and opened her eyes wide. Hugging Ackroyd defensively, she began edging away from Suite 22.

Straight into line with the door of Suite 21. The door swung wide and Evelina T. Carterslee stepped into the corridor.

'Having a spot of bother?' she asked sympathetically. She prided herself that she could pick up any local lingo in no time.

'Just a spot,' Midge said weakly. Through the open doorway, she could see Hermione and Cedric huddled over a table of tea-things. They were waving sheets of typescript at each other and it was obvious that an argument was developing.

'Thought so,' Evelina said triumphantly. 'You should have been warned. Bramwell isn't so bad, but no one in their right minds in the States would have allowed Sweet Amaryllis on the premises.'

'How were we to know?' Midge continued her crabwise progress towards the service stairs. 'We've only read the books. We don't know anything about your private lives.'

'Pity it couldn't have stayed that way, isn't it?' Evelina surveyed her with more than a trace of amusement breaking through her sympathy. 'Never mind, you'll know better next time.'

'Mmm.' Midge refrained from committing herself to any future prospects. She could not resist one question, however.

'Tell me, whatever happened to *Mr* Barbour?'

'Rumour has it—' Evelina's eyes gleamed—'that Sweet Amaryllis ate him soon after mating!'

Ever one to recognize a good exit line, especially when

she had uttered it herself, she stepped back into her suite and closed the door softly behind her.

Midge clawed weakly at the wallpapered panel that gave on to the service stairs. It swung open silently and she stumbled through it, conscious of a great relief at escaping the rarefied atmosphere of Upstairs.

The knives were well and truly out at Chortlesby Manor.

CHAPTER 2

Reggie had tidied the silverware away and the pantry table and counters were now crowded with baking trays waiting to be transferred to the oven when the guests arrived.

Cheese straws, sausage rolls, vol-au-vent shells, miniature pasties, pizzas and quiches Lorraine ought to satisfy the hungry hordes and hold them until dinner-time.

Midge gave an approving nod and continued into the kitchen where Cook sat at the table frowning over her script.

'I'm not sure about this—' Cook looked up. 'Do I throw the apron over my head before I burst into tears or after? It doesn't make sense.'

'I'm sorry about that,' Midge said. 'But cooks were always doing things like that in Golden Age books. You'll just have to do the best you can. Perhaps you can leave one eye free.'

'I don't like it,' Cook said. 'There's enough to do around here without all this nonsense. It makes me look a fool.'

'Well . . .' Midge didn't like to stress the fact that servants were usually considered the comic relief in Thirties novels, they were too hard to get these days. One upset them at one's peril and, as Cook had noted, there was enough to do around here.

'Well,' Midge temporized, 'I think they were often Irish cooks. Probably they had different customs.'

'That's so.' Cook tilted her head to one side, considering.

'I could do that. I wouldn't feel so silly if it wasn't me, like. I'll use an Irish accent then. Begorra.'

'That's fine.' Midge was not about to discourage anything that would keep Cook in a reasonable mood. She took a tighter grip on Ackroyd, who had been restive since spotting the trays of goodies in the pantry. 'Where's Reggie?'

'He's gone into the bar with his little black book,' Cook said, adding darkly, 'Muttering to himself.'

'There's a lot of it about,' Midge muttered and headed for the bar.

It was strategically placed in what had once been a study at the far end of the main drawing-room, so that people could wander out on to the stone-flagged terrace through the French windows in good weather. Alternatively, they could carry their drinks into the drawing-room and settle in the comfortable chairs and sofas in front of the open fire if they didn't want to perch on one of the bar stools in the bar.

'Ah, you got him.' Reggie looked up and nodded a greeting to them both. 'Any problems?'

'Only the usual. She doesn't know what she's doing here and she hates us all.'

'And vice versa, I may say.' Reggie lowered his head again to frown at the recipe book he was studying. 'I hope we're doing the right thing here. Some of these combinations ought to carry a Government health warning. They sound absolutely lethal.'

'I wouldn't be surprised if they were.' Midge perched on a bar stool and let Ackroyd slip to the floor. He sauntered behind the bar to join Reggie. 'Fortunately, we're protected from the worst excesses by the fact that all Governments long ago outlawed absinthe. Pernod isn't nearly so dangerous.'

'In these combinations, I still wouldn't like to take my oath on it.'

'We've done our best.' Midge had spent a morning lettering cards with the names and contents of the cocktails. 'If they want to order the things, on their heads be it.'

'You know they will—out of sheer bravado. And for some

of them, it will be a nostalgia trip. Perhaps we ought to serve them in teacups for the real period atmosphere.'

'Not in England,' Midge corrected. 'We never had Prohibition or speakeasies. That would only be period in the States.'

'I suppose so.' Reggie accepted the correction grumpily. They were all growing a bit weary of the game. It was their first season. Next season it would be easier. For one thing, the 'Guest Stars' would be different—and that alone was bound to be an improvement. Not that Evelina T. Carterslee was so bad; nor even, to be fair, Bramwell. It was Amaryllis who was the genuine worm i' the bud. Perhaps they could insist that only the celebrities be invited—no appendages allowed.

'Well, let's post the warning signals, anyway. Where have you put them?'

'Here.' Reggie reached beneath the counter and slid the stack of cards across the bar. 'And you'll need these.' He added a box of drawing-pins.

'Right!' Midge slid off her stool and took the top card, not by any accident:

American Beauty
1 dash Crème de Menthe
1/4 Orange Juice
1/4 Grenadine
1/4 Dry Vermouth
1/4 Brandy
Topped with Port Wine

'They'll go for the names.' She shook her head forebodingly. 'God knows what it will do to their livers.'

'Relax,' Reggie said. 'Look at all the people who survived the Thirties. And they were smoking their heads off in those days, too. The human race is a lot hardier than it's been currently led to believe it is.'

'It must be.' Midge tacked up the next lethal cocktail beside the first:

> *Bijou*
> 1 dash Orange Bitters
> 1/3 Gin
> 1/3 Green Chartreuse
> 1/3 Vermouth Rosso
> Add a cherry or an olive and a piece of
> lemon peel squeezed on top.

'They're all authentic, remember,' Reggie encouraged her. She was the one who had found the original Thirties book of cocktail recipes. It had seemed like a good idea at the time, now her conscience was beginning to quiver. He nodded as she picked up the next card. 'They'll love that one.'

> *Corpse Reviver*
> 1/4 Vermouth Rosso
> 1/4 Calvados
> 1/2 Cognac

'That's what I'm afraid of.' Midge darted over and tacked it up in a shadowy corner. 'We're the ones who'll have to deal with the aftermath.'

'Post the hangover cure in the centre,' Reggie advised practically. 'That ought to give them the gipsy's warning.'

'All right.' Midge sifted through the cards and came up with the one for pride of place:

> *Prairie Oyster*
> 2 dashes Vinegar
> Unbroken yolk of one Egg
> 1 teaspoonful Worcestershire Sauce
> 1 teaspoonful Tomato Catsup
> 1 dash of Pepper on top
> *To be swallowed at one gulp.*

'If that doesn't discourage them, nothing will,' Reggie said.
'You know nothing will.' Midge gloomily tacked up the next cards:

Merry Widow	*Monkey's Gland*
2 dashes Absinthe	1 dash Absinthe
2 dashes Angostura Bitters	1 teaspoonful Grenadine
2 dashes Benedictine	1/2 Orange Juice
1/2 Dry Vermouth	1/2 Gin
1/2 Gin	

'Then they'll die happy.' Reggie shrugged philosophically.

Royal Romance	*Shamrock*
1/2 Gin	3 dashes Green
1/4 Grand Marnier	Crème de Menthe
1/4 Passion Fruit	3 dashes Green
Juice	Chartreuse
1 dash Grenadine	1/2 Dry Vermouth
	1/2 Irish Whisky

'I'd rather they didn't die here,' Midge said.

'Nonsense girl! Point of the whole thing, isn't it?' Colonel Heather appeared in the entrance to the bar, resplendent in straw boater, blue blazer with silver buttons and white flannel trousers.

'Oh, well done, sir,' Reggie applauded.

'Not bad, eh?' Colonel Heather twirled the ends of his sweeping RAF-style moustache. 'Knew I had something appropriate packed away. Bit out of season, but *they* won't know that, will they?'

'You're perfect!' Midge said warmly. 'You're so perfect, I'm afraid for you. If she can't get you any other way, some rich American widow is going to slip you a mickey and smuggle you away in her luggage.'

'Hah!' The Colonel preened extravagantly. 'And just wait

until you see Grace—Miss Holloway. Done us all proud!'

'I'm sure she has,' Midge said gratefully. It could have been so awkward; they had been afraid it would be. Colonel Heather and Miss Holloway had been resident guests— sitting tenants, as it were—when she and Reggie had taken over Chortlesby Manor last year.

It had rapidly become apparent that the Manor was not paying its way and was never likely to; it was just one more run-of-the-mill country hotel, rapidly sliding downhill. A moot point whether dry rot or bailiffs would get it first. Something drastic had to be done if they were to survive.

But what? Cook, also inherited with the Manor, although honest and willing, was not in the Cordon Bleu class. Nor could they afford to hire a chef able to lift them into the crossed knives and forks, four-Rosette category, even if their financial situation were comfortable enough to allow them to wait upon publishing schedules and the next few tourist seasons to establish a more-than-passing trade.

The current trade had been just about nil. Reggie's father, with typical hopeful improvidence, had taken out a mort-gage and turned the Manor into a hotel with the intention of saving the family homestead and earning a neat profit.

Alas, poor Eric. There were more stately mansions in too close a proximity, quainter hostelries spread their Tudor wings along coach roads and more luxuriously-appointed modern hotels offered centrally-heated comfort in the centre of town. The Manor, although beloved by generations of Chortlesbys, had little to offer those who were not already among the converted.

Eric had taken on the competition by shaving his running costs to the bone and offering the lowest prices possible. It had attracted the transient trade and, perhaps unfortu-nately, a cluster of permanent residents, mostly elderly. In those days, Eric had been too new to the game to see the pitfalls in this.

One fractured hip, two cases of pneumonia, one senile dementia and two deaths later, Eric had learned far more than he had ever wanted to know about the problems of running a residential hotel.

By this time, Eric had felt that he was faced with the loss of either the Manor or his mind. He called a family conference and faced them with the problems. They were unanimous that, whatever else might be lost, Chortlesby Manor must be preserved.

Reggie, as heir presumptive, had agreed to leave his post in the City and take over as proprietor of the Manor/hotel. Midge, as his loving wife and presumptive mother of future heirs, could do no less than agree to the proposal, although, with Eric a healthy specimen of a long-lived line, she had not reckoned on being called to take over any duties as Lady of the Manor for a good many years yet—by which time she had hoped that she would have a better idea of what she ought to be doing.

Aunt Hermione and her husband, Cedric, Eric's sister and brother-in-law, had nobly volunteered to leave their rural retreat and move in to help with the housekeeping and gardening, respectively. This had begun to seem slightly less noble when they had promptly rented their cottage to an American exchange professor for an exorbitant price he, in his innocence, considered the bargain of the decade. They had then taken up rent-free residence at the Manor, although, to give them their due, they pulled their full weight, and then some.

Cook was a constant, no matter what changes they rang in on her, and assorted girls from the surrounding country-side did part-time work as maids and waitresses under Hermione's expert tuition.

With the domestic arrangements thus ensured, Eric had blessed them all and thankfully departed for a long recuperative visit to distant relatives in Australia, murmuring cheerful hopes of finding business ventures which would restore the family fortunes. They had all bade him a fond farewell, then settled down grimly to some restoration work of their own.

Bunny Hug
1/3 Gin
1/3 Scotch
1/3 Absinthe
(Not Recommended)

'I should think not.' Colonel Heather winced as he read the next card Midge tacked up. 'Bunny Hug, eh? Sounds more like a boa constrictor to me.'

'That's very good,' Reggie chuckled. 'Be sure to repeat it when the guests arrive. Ought to get a good laugh, put them in the right mood.'

'Will do.' The Colonel preened again. 'Wizard script this time round, I might say. Ought to keep the beggars guessing, what?'

'We certainly hope so.' Midge tacked up the last card, giving it pride of place.

Luigi
2 dashes Grenadine
1 dash Cointreau
Juice of half a Tangerine
1/2 Gin
1/2 Dry Vermouth

'Oh dear,' she said. 'I do hope Mrs Carterslee doesn't feel honour-bound to keep ordering that all weekend just because it's the name of her series character.'

'Don't see how she can avoid it,' the Colonel pointed out practically. 'The fans are sure to keep buying it for her. Tempted to, myself.' He gave the short sharp bark that served him for a laugh. 'Wait till Sweet Amaryllis sees that. She'll demand equal time for Bramwell's characters.'

'Fortunately, we haven't found any cocktails with those names,' Midge said.

'Doubt if that will save you. Ignorance is no excuse, and all that. She'll probably insist you invent a couple on the spot.'

'That's an idea,' Reggie said. 'Maybe we could have an Invent a Cocktail Contest. Turn them loose behind the bar and let them have at it.'

'Let's keep that one in reserve,' Midge said. 'It sounds too much like something that could turn into an utter shambles. Perhaps we could just invite Bramwell to invent a cocktail instead.'

'Anything so long as he gets equal time,' Colonel Heather barked again. 'If you ask me, Evelina is the one who ought to have more time. There are two of them and only one of her.'

'It won't happen again,' Midge said grimly. 'I'll make certain of that.'

'Good show!' The Colonel sketched a salute. 'I'll leave you to it now. Got to find Grace. We're cooking up a few red herrings for the party.'

'That's awfully good of you,' Midge said gratefully. 'But you do so much already and, really, you needn't do anything at all. Just lurk around and look suspicious. You lurk so beautifully.'

'My pleasure,' he said handsomely. 'Grace's, too. Given her a whole new lease on life, this murder lark. Made a new woman of her.'

It hadn't done so badly by the Colonel, either. Midge smiled at his retreating back. They had been so lucky there. The main reason for trepidation as they launched their new venture was the attitude of the remaining permanent residents.

How would they react to *Murder at the Manor?*

CHAPTER 3

For they had explored every avenue and it seemed that murder was their only salvation.

Even so, the opportunity had come more through luck

than judgement. Through Midge's school Newsletter to Old Girls, in fact.

Midge had sent in a paragraph about the exciting new life she and Reggie had embarked on as proprietors of the lovely old Chortlesby Manor Hotel situated in the beautiful Wiltshire countryside but within comfortable distance of picturesque Salisbury, for those who preferred city life. There had been a discreet hint that favourable terms would be extended to Old Girls who might like to book weekend breaks or holidays.

It was a bow drawn at venture. The best Midge had hoped for had been a few weekend bookings from bargain-hunting and/or curious ex-schoolmates.

What she got was a trans-Atlantic telephone call from Victoria Ransome.

They had been good but not particularly close friends at school. After leaving, inevitably their paths drifted apart. The Newsletter had informed all Old Girls that Victoria had emigrated to the United States and, later, that she had opened a book shop, The Crimson Shroud, specializing in crime and mystery books, both new and old, in Boston, Massachusetts.

Now, Victoria was on the trans-Atlantic line with an offer they couldn't refuse.

'Murder at the Manor,' Victoria said. 'It's a natural. I've been thinking of it for some time. A lot of the mystery bookshops over here are running their own tours and my customers have been telling me it's high time I organized one for them. They're afraid they're missing out on all the fun. I think so, too. When I read about your hotel, it sounded ideal. It *is* small enough for an intimate gathering, isn't it?'

'We have three suites,' Midge said proudly, 'and twenty-three bedrooms, four of them occupied by resident guests. That's not counting the family quarters and rooms for the living-in help.'

'Perfect!' Victoria enthused. 'I *knew* it was right, as soon as I saw the item. Look, I'll have to get back to you on this

—I'm negotiating a tie-up with Roberta Rinehart and her Death On Wheels Bookshop in California—but I'll provisionally charter Chortlesby Manor for three alternate weekends, say mid-January through end-February. And we'll book two suites for the full run of six weeks for our resident authors—it will be cheaper than paying their air fares each weekend.'

'Just a minute—' Midge was delighted, but dizzy. 'You're losing me.'

'Oh no, I'm not,' Victoria assured her. 'I'm going to hold on to you very tightly. You're just what I've been looking for. You needn't worry about a thing. I'll hire the actors over there. We'll need rooms for them, three or four—we might as well engage them for the six weeks, too. They'll be able to go up to London midweek, if they like, but basically they can treat it as a repertory engagement.'

'We ought to be able to manage that.' Midge tried to say it calmly. Beside her, Reggie was nodding so vigorously he nearly dislodged the telephone from her hand. Two suites and three, possibly four, rooms let for six weeks was going to carry them through the depths of the Off-Season; not to mention having the Manor chartered for three weekends. She still wasn't quite sure what Victoria was talking about but, never mind, the bookings proposed would set them well on the road to solvency.

'Here's your cold tea.' Cook set a large jug of pale amber liquid down on the bar counter. 'And I've put the bottle of blood behind the cooker to warm up. Her Ladyship complained it was too cold last time. Says she nearly caught a chill.'

'That's fine.' Reggie poured the cold tea into the waiting crystal decanter and placed it on the shelf beneath the bar. It would be used for most of the drinks ordered by the actors and also for most of those offered to Colonel Heather and Miss Holloway by the other guests. Not because of any intention to defraud the Americans who vied to buy drinks for such splendidly English specimens, but because so much trans-Atlantic generosity threatened to put the Colonel and Miss Holloway under the table before the party even started.

'There's another jug of tea in the fridge,' Cook said gloomily, having learned early on the first weekend that the drinks were going to disappear like rain into the parched earth after a drought.

They had all learned a lot that first weekend.

'No, please—' Miss Holloway had demurred piteously, as yet another large American gentleman tried to press yet another large drink upon her. 'I couldn't. I really couldn't. I've had so much—too much—already. I simply couldn't. Thank you just the same, but—no! Definitely not!'

'Aw, come on, honey—' He had beckoned Reggie forward imperiously. 'Let the bartender get you just one more.'

'No, please—'

'I insist. It's my turn to interrogate you, and you know what they say. *In vino veritas.* Unless—' He leered down at her hopefully. 'Unless you're of the Adam MacAdam persuasion—'

'No! No!' Miss Holloway had whooped hysterically. 'I'll have a double gin! And tonic! Lots of tonic—'

'That's more like it.' But there had been a trace of disappointment in the broad friendly face. The hour was late, the lights were low, and Grace Holloway had been blossoming all evening under the unaccustomed attention.

'Here you are!' Reggie had set the bubbling goblet down in front of her, with a wink of his offside eye.

'Thank you—' She picked it up and sipped reluctantly. Her relieved smile had brightened that corner of the bar as she realized that there was only tonic, ice and a slice of lemon in the glass. 'That's splendid. That's just the job!'

'Thank you, miss,' Reggie had said noncommittally and retreated as her escort leaned forward and began shooting questions at her. When next he signalled and Reggie darted forward, Miss Holloway had been in command of the situation.

'Same again,' she had said firmly, handing him her glass. 'Please.'

Later, Colonel Heather had somehow twigged the game and, upon being offered another drink, had said to Reggie with a meaning look, 'I'll have what the little lady is having.'

Reggie had been only too delighted to comply. It had set the pattern for the rest of that weekend and for future weekends. Later, Midge and Reggie had discussed it and, after the weekend guests had departed, had slipped discreet envelopes beneath Colonel Heather and Miss Holloway's respective doors, containing a share of the bar proceeds on their drinks.

Miss Holloway had demurred at first, but the Colonel had been frankly amused. 'We had a name for the girls out East who did this sort of thing,' he said. 'Little did I ever think I'd be doing it myself one day. But the world turns, the world turns . . .'

'I can't think it's right,' Miss Holloway protested feebly. 'I feel sinful enough about fooling those poor generous people in the first place, but I simply couldn't manage all those drinks—'

'Nonsense, Grace, take the money and be thankful,' the Colonel ordered. 'You can't deny it will come in useful.'

Miss Holloway did not attempt to deny it. When one's pension wasn't index-linked, every little bit helped. Blushing, she had stowed it away in her handbag almost guiltily, but over the next few weeks she had made a rapid adjustment to the new circumstances. Only yesterday, she had returned from town with a black velvet suit she had merrily announced was 'the Wages of Sin'.

'There.' Reggie finished polishing the straight-sided cocktail glasses and lined them up behind the bar. It was fortunate that there had been an Art Deco Revival lately and the Thirties-style cocktail glasses were in open stock once more. It saved any worry about replacing broken or chipped glasses. 'Ready and waiting. Let them come! Everything all right with your end of things?'

'Tickety-boo, as the Colonel would say.' Midge nodded with satisfaction. A lucky find at a local jumble sale just after New Year had provided a hoard of Thirties magazines and newspapers, which had sparked the idea for this final weekend. Now the magazines had been strategically distributed throughout the public rooms and the newspapers were piled in the kitchen waiting to be utilized to the best advantage. 'They're going to feel as though they've slipped through a time-warp.'

'That's what they're paying for.' Reggie untied his apron and tossed it over his arm. 'Well, then, I think we're as ready as we ever are.'

'Just the same, I'm glad it's the last one.' Midge sighed faintly. 'It's an awful lot of work.'

'That's why they pay so well.' Reggie tipped back the hinged panel of the bar counter and stepped out to join her. 'Besides—' he put his arm around her shoulders and gave her a quick squeeze—'it hasn't been so bad, has it?'

'Sometimes it's been fun,' she admitted. 'If only—'

'I know. If they want to sign up the Manor for another series of weekends, we'll make it a condition that the resident authors are orphans.'

'*And* she's playing up again,' Midge was reminded. 'She doesn't want Bramwell to take part in any of the festivities this weekend. He mustn't be disturbed. It seems he's reached a crucial part of his book. Adam MacAdam and Suzie Chong are about to start interrogating the suspects.'

'What?' Reggie reacted with the same affronted horror Midge had felt. 'Under *our* roof?'

'Take it easy.' Midge had recovered from her own initial shock and could laugh now. 'They're not real, you know.'

'I know,' Reggie admitted ruefully. 'But the way all these people talk about them, one tends to forget that.'

'I don't,' Midge said. 'I often thank heaven for it. Imagine if those ghastly characters had been real and we were stuck with them here for six weeks.'

'It's nearly as bad just having their creators,' Reggie said. 'I'm not so sure—' a mischievous spark glinted in his eyes —'I'd object to Suzie Chong.'

'No, but I would!'

Once the arrangements had been final, they had rushed to the library to read up on their about-to-be-resident authors and become familiar with their works. Both authors had been writing for well over a decade and maintained flourishing series characters with large followings.

Bramwell Barbour was the creator of that sprightly multi-ethnic husband-and-wife detecting team, Adam MacAdam, the American-Scottish mulatto and his beautiful French-Eurasian wife, Suzie Chong. In keeping with the spirit of certain lifestyles prevelant in this last quarter of the Twentieth Century, the MacAdams maintained a marriage so open a juggernaut lorry could have been driven through it without touching either partner.

Their most baffling and blood-curdling cases invariably devolved into sexual romps, due to Suzie's theory (heartily endorsed by Adam) that *veritas* resided not *in vino* but in bed. When it came time for serious interrogation of the suspects, they divided the chore, Suzie sliding off to sleep with the main male suspects, while Adam handled (literally) the female suspects. (Thus far, Bramwell Barbour had not extended his excursions into the Permissive Society to the point of including any homosexual suspects.) Later, much later, they lay back together in their massive water bed, exhausted (although not by each other), and compared notes on the results of their questioning. Inevitably, they solved the case, although it was sometimes necessary to re-interrogate the suspects, sometimes jointly. (The enormous water bed gave a new twist to the gathering of the suspects for the final solution.) At some point on the last page, one of the cleared suspects, with a twinkle in his or her eye, invariably voiced the recurring tag line: 'It was a pleasure being suspected by you.'

Reviewers had been ecstatic from the very first appearance of Adam MacAdam and Suzie Chong in *Death On Wheels*. One reviewer had gone so far as to proclaim them: 'Mr and Mrs North, as they would have been if they were being written today.' His newspaper had promptly been threatened with a lawsuit by the Lockridge Estate for Defamation of Characters. The apology and retraction had gone so far in the opposite direction that Bramwell Barbour had then sued for damages. Another grovelling apology and retraction had followed, plus a substantial out-of-Court settlement. The luckless reviewer, who had wisely hidden behind the pseudonym 'The Sphinx', had last been heard of writing a newsletter for an electricity company in Upstate New York.

Evelina T. Carterslee, on the other hand, had cleverly sidestepped the entire issue of sex by making her multi-ethnic detective, Luigi von Murphy, a failed Trappist monk. Although he had leapt over the wall in other respects (there was a strong hint that his health was responsible for his defection), he had continued to feel bound by his vow of celibacy, despite the best—or worst—hopes of susceptible females he encountered in the course of his investigations. Since his debut in *The Crimson Shroud*, he had gathered a large and devoted following, many of whom eagerly pounced on each new book hoping that this would be the one in which Luigi's Latin blood would win out over his Nordic reserve and Irish scruples. They were still waiting—and hoping.

Remote and austere, Luigi von Murphy trod alone through the maze of suspicion and accusation, judging that he be judged not, but watching, noting, drawing conclusions. At moments, he would draw himself up sharply with a gasp that might have been of realization or of pain. (Evelina T. Carterslee had to reassure her readers periodically that Luigi's health, although frail, was not perilous.)

At last, he would retire to the laboratory of his cottage

on the Connecticut shore, don his old monk's habit and concentrate his mind by distilling his own liqueurs. He could also brew up a mean kettle of jam. To the intense regret of his many fans, he also considered himself bound by his vows of silence when asked for the recipes.

Rarely, very rarely, one of the ladies in a case made such an impression on him that he could only exorcize it by creating a new scent in her honour. (To Evelina's intense annoyance, no perfume manufacturer had yet taken the hint.)

By the time they had read the complete works of both authors, Ackroyd was the only inhabitant of Chortlesby Manor who was not in a state of ill-controlled panic at the prospect of their imminent arrival.

It had come as a great relief to discover that Bramwell Barbour was not a rampaging satyr and that Evelina T. Carterslee was not particularly religious.

Their relief was short-lived, however. The next afternoon, Bramwell borrowed the car and went to the station to meet the train from London. He returned with Amaryllis.

Into each life some rain must fall, but it was generally agreed that Bramwell carried his own monsoon around with him. The weather at Chortlesby Manor had been stormy ever since her arrival.

Perhaps the most irritating thing was that Amaryllis fawned on Bramwell's fans and was generally regarded by them as charming. She was at her most obnoxious with members of the staff and, of course, the actors.

CHAPTER 4

'By the way—' Midge was reminded. 'Where's Lettie?'

'Lettie? She and Ned took the car into town to try to find more feathers for the head-dresses. They ought to be back any minute now.'

As well as being the 'Screamer', the maid who discovered the bodies, Lettie doubled as Props, assembling and keeping track of the various props needed in the enactments. She was also stage-managing the productions—no easy task when the 'stage' sprawled throughout almost the entire Manor. Only the private quarters of family and staff and the kitchen were out of bounds.

Nor was it easy to attempt to co-ordinate actors who had been given the mere skeleton of a script and were expected to flesh out the bones themselves. It was Method acting at its most challenging. Fun, but exhausting—with more complications than were ever encountered on a real stage.

However, the money was good, the food excellent and the accommodation superb. At this season of the year, the alternative would have been a provincial pantomime, living in cheap digs in some distant outpost. A further bonus was the enthusiastic and appreciative audience.

'Sorry—' a voice called out as the front door slammed.

'Lettie never misses a cue,' Reggie said admiringly.

'Even when she doesn't know she's just had one,' Midge agreed.

Ackroyd strolled out from behind the bar and stretched at their feet with an elaborately casual air that deceived no one. Lettie had never yet failed to return from town without some special treat for him. His head turned towards the doorway expectantly as the hurrying footsteps drew nearer.

'They haven't arrived yet, have they?' Lettie swept in, precariously clutching a pile of slipping parcels and deposited them on the bar counter. 'Oh, it's so nice and warm in here. It's bitter out—and I think we're going to have some snow. They'll love that. Bags of atmosphere.'

'We aim to please,' Reggie said. 'But I'll bet it's not half so popular as the fog we had last month.'

'That *was* a stroke of luck,' Lettie agreed. 'And here's another.' She began emptying bags. 'Look—treasure trove!' She uptilted a bag and spilled a cascade of green and white Penguin paperbacks across the counter.

'Oh, super!' Midge squealed. 'We were running low. Where did you find them?'

'The local Oxfam. Someone had obviously had a great clear-out and I got there at just the right moment.'

'Three Agatha Christies, two Margery Allinghams, Ngaio Marsh, John Dickson Carr, Gladys Mitchell, Elizabeth Ferrars, Michael Innes . . .' Midge gloated unashamedly over the haul. 'Oh, these are super!'

'I don't know all that much about it,' Lettie said, 'but I'm learning. I recognized those green and white covers—and I just grabbed. I knew we could use them.'

'We certainly can,' Midge said heartily. From the first tour, they had tried to make the guests feel at home by leaving an assortment of vintage mystery paperbacks by the bed in each room. The gesture had gone down well. The only problem was that the guests assumed—or pretended to assume—that the paperbacks were a little present from the Manor. When they departed, the paperbacks were packed into their cases and taken away with them. (At least, it cut down on the disappearance rate of ashtrays and towels.) After that first tour, they had reduced the number of paperbacks in each room from six to three. Fortunately, there was a plentiful source of supply in the local charity shops and jumble sales, so long as no one was a purist about first editions.

'And there are four hardbacks in this bag.' Lettie lifted them out carefully. 'All Thirties imprints, although I don't know any of these authors. I thought we could leave them lying around the lounge to dress the house—'

Ackroyd had had enough. He leaped up on the nearest bar stool and rested his forepaws on the counter. He butted his head against Lettie's hand impatiently.

'Oh, you!' She ruffled his soft white front. 'I suppose you think I've brought you something?'

'He knows very well you have,' Midge said. 'You spoil him rotten.'

'Well, you're worth spoiling, aren't you?' Lettie smoothed

the white ruff, running her fingers down into the tiger markings of Ackroyd's back. Ackroyd blinked his large yellow eyes and purred loudly. His long white whiskers twitched expectantly.

'All right.' Lettie opened her handbag and pulled out a small white bag. Ackroyd was rubbing his nose against it before she had it free of the handbag. He uttered loud cries of approval.

'All right, take it easy.' Lettie pulled away, laughing, as Ackroyd began pawing wildly at the bag. 'Let me open it for you.'

Ackroyd assured her that wasn't necessary, he'd just shred it himself.

'What on earth have you got there?' Midge asked. 'Look at him—he's going mad.'

'Catnip will do it every time—*ow*!' Lettie dropped the bag as a claw grazed her hand. The bag fell to the floor and Ackroyd leaped down after it.

'You needn't have been so rough about it.' Lettie feinted a light kick towards him. 'I was giving it to you, anyway.'

'He's only about a year old,' Midge apologized. 'He goes wild with excitement.'

'Big for his age, isn't he?' Lettie watched as Ackroyd caught the paper bag between his forepaws and somersaulted with it.

'Not surprising,' Reggie said. 'He eats like a horse.'

'So would you,' Midge said, 'if you'd had his start in life. Remember how scrawny he was when he came to us?'

There was a moment's pause as they both remembered the starveling kitten who had suddenly appeared at the back door one day soon after they had taken over management of the Manor. No human being could have resisted giving it a drink of milk and a saucer of scraps.

From that first instant, Ackroyd had had no doubt as to his place in the world. They had hesitated only because they had feared prospective guests might be put off by a resident cat. Some might be allergic, some might want to bring their dogs along. While the debate raged, Ackroyd curled up and went to sleep in a corner of a sofa by the fire and the outside temperature abruptly dropped by ten degrees. It could not do any harm to let him spend one night in the warmth of the kitchen.

When they went down in the morning, a furry throbbing dynamo hurled itself at their legs, uttering cries of welcome and delight, then proudly led them to a corner where a rat lay dead—a rat nearly as big as he was. He wasn't just a freeloader, the kitten let them know proudly, he could work his passage.

And so Ackroyd had joined the staff of Chortlesby Manor. Not that he was Ackroyd at first. He had begun as Roger the Lodger, progressing to Roger Ackroyd when they had begun contemplating Murder at the Manor. Whatever they called him, Ackroyd was agreeable. He had disposed of more rats and mice than they had ever suspected inhabited the Manor and won the hearts of Cook and the remaining residents. Chortlesby Manor inserted a note to their listing in hotel directories that dogs were not allowed. Ackroyd had full run of the Manor, including all the public rooms and most of the bedrooms.

He was taking full advantage now. A mighty swipe had knocked the plump grey catnip mouse out of the bag and Ackroyd leaped for it with a hunting cry. It skittered away from him, through the doorway, into the front hall. Ackroyd raced after it, wild-eyed and rowdy.

There was a crash and a scream.

They dashed outside to find Amaryllis Barbour sitting on the lowest step of the stairs, rubbing her ankle.

'That animal tripped me!' she said. The telltale mouse lay abandoned at her feet. Ackroyd had withdrawn to the far end of the lobby and watched unblinking.

'I'm terribly sorry, Mrs Barbour.' Midge came forward. 'Lettie just gave Ackroyd a catnip mouse. He's never seen one before. I'm afraid he got over-excited.' She stooped and retrieved the mouse, tossing it to Reggie, who caught it deftly and slipped it into his pocket.

'Hmmphh!' Amaryllis Barbour swept Ackroyd, Reggie, Midge and Lettie with a look which consigned them all to the nethermost regions. Especially Lettie.

'Are you all right? Can you stand up?' Midge took her arm and gently urged her to her feet.

'It's no thanks to you I haven't broken my neck!' Amaryllis groaned as she straightened up. 'If you *must* have animals, they should be banned from the public rooms. That cat will be the death of someone yet!'

'No such luck,' Lettie muttered under her breath.

'There.' Midge shot Lettie a silencing look. 'There, now, you're all right. No harm done—'

'There better not be!' Amaryllis seemed in a worse mood than usual. Unfortunately, there was a certain amount of justice on her side at the moment.

'Were you going to town?' Midge offered hasty distraction. 'Ned is still out at the car. I'm sure he'd be willing to run you in—'

'On the contrary, Ned's right here.' He appeared round the corner, car keys dangling from his hand. 'However, I'd be quite happy to drive you—'

'No, thank you. Just give me the keys.' Amaryllis held out her hand imperiously. 'I prefer to drive myself.'

'As you wish.' Ned extended the keys and she snatched them from him.

There was silence as she marched across the lobby and stalked out, slamming the door behind her.

'*I prefer to drive myself*,' Lettie mimicked, catching the voice and intonation so well that, had anyone had their eyes closed, they could have believed it was Amaryllis herself speaking. 'When she's not driving Bramwell, that is!'

'Poor Old Bramwell.' Ned sauntered over. 'If you had half a heart, Lettie, you'd marry the poor devil and take him away from all that.'

'Half a heart—and no brain! Who'd want to get tied up with a mother-in-law like that?'

'I shouldn't think you'd find it too hard to persuade him to stay on in England—and ship Mother Barbour back to the States. I'd put my money on you any day.'

'Better not let Sweet Amaryllis hear you making suggestions like that—or you could wind up a real-life victim,' Reggie warned.

'I doubt if she'd need that much excuse to get rid of him —or any of us—if the mood took her,' Lettie said. 'She hates all actors. She thinks we're rogues, vagabonds—and probably thieves. Have you seen the way she clutches her handbag when any of us come into the room?'

'Oh, I think you're exaggerating.' Actually, Midge *had* noticed, but she'd hoped the actors hadn't.

'Stop giving her the benefit of the doubt!' Lettie said. 'I should think you'd be as fed up with her as we are. More so. All she ever does is whinge and complain—'

'Careful!' Reggie broke in. 'Someone's coming.'

They glanced upwards guiltily, then with one accord moved into the lounge. Just inside the door, they halted.

A strange little figure slumped in a chair beside the dying fire. Her head turned questingly towards them.

'Hell!' Reggie muttered. 'When did she arrive? Is she part of the tour or—'

'I'm terribly sorry,' Midge apologized. 'We didn't mean to disturb you. We didn't realize anyone was—'

'Oh, well played, Grace!' Lettie applauded. 'You'll be a sensation!'

'Do you think so?' Miss Holloway glowed. 'I thought— a little local colour—'

She was wearing a shapeless grey cardigan and skirt, a lace fichu at her throat. A bag of knitting lay beside the chair.

'You're a perfect period piece,' Lettie said. 'We'll have to watch them that they don't try to take you home with them.'

'I *did* think it might add something to the weekend,' Grace Holloway murmured modestly.

'It's a splendid effort.' Midge moved through the room, snapping on the lamps. Approaching dusk and the gathering storm had made the day even darker than was usual at this hour. As the room began to spring to life, Miss Holloway took on less of a ghostly appearance. Even the fire seemed to revive.

'They should be here soon.' Reggie threw more wood on the fire and poked at it, then looked around approvingly. 'That looks more welcoming.'

'And tea and toasted scones as soon as they arrive.' Grace Holloway gave a small sigh of contentment. 'Who could ask for anything more?'

'*I got rhythm* . . .' From the doorway, someone took up the song cue.

'*I got music* . . .' The Honourable Petronella Van Dine Charlestoned to the centre of the lounge and struck a pose. Three white aigret plumes trembled in her headband as she swung her head to survey the lounge and demanded:

'But where's my man? Where's Algie? Where, oh where, is my darling Algie?' She clasped her hands girlishly in front of her. 'I will *never* believe all those dreadful stories about him. They are foul lies put about by his enemies. Nothing will ever convince me that my darling Algernon Moriarty is a villain!'

'Okay . . .' Lettie drawled critically. 'But take it down half an octave or you'll have no voice left by the end of the weekend.'

'Nothing will ever—' Petronella began obediently, half an octave lower.

'Not now. Save it for the paying customers.'

'Where *is* . . . Algie?' Midge asked. It had seemed strange at first, but now it was almost natural to call them all by the names they used in their scenarios. The only difficulty was keeping track of them. Fortunately, Hermione and

Cedric, now that they were so enthusiastically a part of the proceedings, had been written in under their own names. Otherwise, it might have been a bit of a problem in general conversation.

'He's around somewhere,' Lettie said carelessly.

'But oughtn't he to be here now?'

'Don't worry. It will be all right on the night.'

'Don't look now—' Reggie turned away from the window —'but night has just fallen.'

'Ohmigawd!' Lettie abruptly lost her casual air. She dashed to the window and peered out.

In the carriageway, a chartered coach was discharging its passengers. They clustered together in small groups, staring up at the imposing grey stone mass of Chortlesby Manor. Some of them clutched pieces of paper in their hands.

'They're here!' Lettie cried. 'They're early!'

'Not terribly,' Midge said, watching her old school friend stride up the wide stone steps. 'You'd better get to the door.' She dredged her mind for the proper phrase and produced it triumphantly as the doorbell pealed. 'You're on!'

A few of the passengers were now moving towards the entrance, but most were hanging back, desperately devouring the information on their sheets of paper as though they were about to sit an examination.

CHAPTER 5

You are cordially invited to
MURDER AT THE MANOR
Theme: Choice of Heir to Van Dine Industries

As an American, you are either a high-ranking executive or major shareholder of Van Dine Industries. Old Ellery

Van Dine has peacefully breathed his last at the age of ninety-four, in this year of grace, 1935. In his Last Will and Testament, he clearly stated that he wished his own flesh and blood to inherit his vast fortune and Van Dine Industries. He further stipulated that his heir must take personal control of Van Dine Industries, since he felt that only a member of the family could properly guide the fortunes of the firm through these difficult times.

There are two candidates: his great-grand-daughter, the **Honourable Petronella Van Dine** and his great nephew, **Edwin Lupin.**

As old Ellery had seen neither of his prospective heirs since they were children, he left it up to you, the executives and shareholders of Van Dine Industries, to decide between them.

The Hon. Petronella Van Dine was brought up on a tea plantation in Ceylon, to which her father had retired after his young wife's death in a road accident. He blamed himself for the accident because he had lost control of his Dusenburg and collided with a Bugatti after a night's gambling (during which he had lost heavily) at the Casino in Monte Carlo.

Petronella had assumed her mother's maiden name in order to inherit her mother's estate and had accompanied her father to Ceylon. She had been sent to an English-run boarding-school in Madras, returning to the tea plantation for holidays. But Petronella has grown up and must be allowed to take her rightful place in Society, so her father has sent her to England to be Presented at Court under the ægis of his old friend . . .

Lady Hermione Marsh, who has quietly evolved a thriving business guiding Provincial and Colonial young ladies through the intricacies of Society. Despite her best efforts, however, Petronella has become known to the Press as the Madcap Heiress, blotted her copybook by refusing to dance with the Prince of Wales (because he kept watching a certain Mrs Simpson all the time he was talking to

Petronella), and compounded these felonies by falling in love with . . .

Lieutenant Algernon (Algie) Moriarty, known far and wide as the Cad of the Regiment, whose debts to every tailor in Savile Row were exceeded only by his Mess bills. He had recently been discovered elbow-deep in the Regimental funds and left alone in his study with a revolver containing one bullet so that he could do the honourable thing. As soon as the door had closed behind his friends, Algie had decamped through the window, subsequently pawning the revolver. (He had later been heard to grumble that he could have got a better price had there been a full clip of bullets in it.) Unfortunately, the face he shows Petronella is a convincing one and she refuses to believe any of the rumours circulating about him.

Reeling under these blows, Lady Hermione has withdrawn the Hon. Petronella from the social swim, hoping that the scandals may fade from the public mind if they lie low for a while. To this end, she has retreated with Petronella to Chortlesby Manor, home of her brother . . .

Sir Cedric Strangeways, military historian, currently working on a magnum opus of the Great War. To aid him in his research, he has a constant stream of houseguests, come to impart their reminiscences of battles and events of the Great War (1914–1918). He has welcomed his sister and her protégée, but his heart—and most of his attention—remains in the past. He has cheerfully opened his Manor to the Van Dine contingent, although perhaps not quite sure of the purpose of your visit.

By sheer coincidence, Edwin (Ned) Lupin has chosen to spend this year of grace (1935) studying at Oxford University. He has been summoned to Chortlesby Manor by the Van Dine solicitor so that you may have the opportunity of meeting him, studying him and comparing him with Petronella Van Dine and deciding which of them you would find it easier to work with. Edwin is a fine, upstanding, all-American boy who appears to have no vices—none that have been discovered, so far. Is he, perhaps, too perfect?

You have the weekend to ponder your decision. It will not be all work and no play, however. On Saturday morning, transport will be provided for those of you who might wish to explore Salisbury and visit the Cathedral. We will be having a Scavenger Hunt on Saturday afternoon and a Gala Dinner on Saturday evening.

Undoubtedly, there will be other events of interest to test your judgement and business acumen. In the case of untoward events, please consult the notice board in the lobby, where necessary information will be posted.

We trust that your visit to Chortlesby Manor will be an enjoyable and memorable one.

We also trust that you will come to the right decision as to the fittest heir/ess to your own Van Dine Industries.

CHAPTER 6

The front door swung open and the first guests advanced hesitantly into the lobby. Out of the corner of her eye, Midge saw Pet and Algie slip through the French windows on to the terrace and disappear in the direction of the kitchen, safely out of sight of any of the guests.

'Welcome to Chortlesby Manor!' Beaming impartially upon them all, Midge swept forward to brush cheeks with Victoria Ransome.

Behind Victoria, the tour members milled in an amorphous mass. Some faces smiled, some were carefully blank, some frowned. Twenty complete strangers, birds of passage alighting at Chortlesby Manor for forty-eight-odd hours. Midge had learned from experience that some of the strangers would emerge into personalities over the next few hours, but others would inevitably remain part of the background, too tired or too indifferent to make an effort to impress themselves upon this alien scene, already looking forward only to the end of their wanderings and their return to their own homes and the lives they had left in abeyance for the duration of the tour. Some would throw themselves into the weekend as their last fling before returning to mundane life, others would regard it as just something to be endured before they could take up their proper place in the world again.

'Pleasant journey?' Midge inquired, as Victoria stepped back and ran a practised eye over her charges.

'Pleasant enough,' Victoria said absently. She looked pale and weary. Midge wondered fleetingly if she were on the point of illness, there was a lot of 'flu around.

'It's so nice to be back here. This place is beginning to feel like home. Or perhaps—' Victoria sighed faintly—'it's the thought that I'm handing over to someone else for a few days. This trip seems to have lasted longer than usual.'

'It's a lot,' Midge said. 'Three tours in six weeks. You're not a professional courier. You just leave everything to us for the weekend and have a good rest.'

'I wish I could, but I'm going back to London with the coach. I have some book-buying to do for the shop. I'll be back for the Gala Dinner tomorrow.' She hesitated. 'You don't mind, do you?'

'No, no, not at all.' Midge fought down a rising sense of panic. What could possibly go wrong? 'We're all prepared for Murder at the Manor. It's a new script this time. I'm just sorry you won't be here to see it.'

'I'll be back for most of it. You're doing the big scene at the Gala Dinner, aren't you?'

'One of them,' Midge said. 'The other one is tonight. After dinner seems to be the best point for them—and then it takes care of the rest of the evening for those who aren't interested in dancing.'

'Which is most of them. The women always seem to outnumber the men on every tour I've ever seen and ours is no exception.'

'They look happy and lively.' Midge watched them as

they mobbed the reception desk, registering and accepting their room keys from Reggie.

'They're that, all right—and they've been looking forward to this weekend. It's the grande finale of their tour and, I warn you, we've got at least half a dozen who are determined to solve the case on their own. We'll be lucky if they don't come to blows with each other.'

'That ought to add to the fun.' The front door stood wide open as the coach driver carried suitcases inside and placed them in neat rows opposite the reception desk.

Ackroyd stalked into the lobby and glared disapprovingly at the open door. He hated draughts. In response to coos and clicking noises, he turned and surveyed the tour coldly. He was not too pleased about them, either.

'Here, kitty . . . here, kitty . . .' Several cat-lovers tried to tempt him to them.

'His name is Ackroyd,' Reggie said.

'Ackroyd . . .' someone pondered aloud. 'Is that a clue?'

'I see what you mean.' Midge turned away to hide a smile. 'They *are* keen.'

'Some of them are absolutely manic. At least, that's my own opinion.' Victoria frowned. 'I did tell you, didn't I, that these aren't our regulars. A few of them are, but most of them came on the first two tours and we had to cast our net wider to fill all the places on this one. We advertised in the Book Pages of some Sunday newspapers and got enough applicants to bring us up to a break-even point. They're all right, but they're not mixing as well as I'd hoped with the regulars.'

'Ackroyd . . . here, Ackroyd . . .' The most persistent were still trying. Ackroyd turned his back on them, flicked up his tail, twitched the tip of it and marched off.

'Your cat isn't very friendly,' a woman complained to Reggie.

'He will be when he gets to know you,' Reggie said.

'I wouldn't bet on that,' the woman said. She seemed surprised when several people laughed.

'You'll see.' Reggie handed her her key quickly and raised his voice. 'Tea will be served in the Residents' Lounge in half an hour.'

The lobby was clearing as the tour collected their suitcases and strayed off to find their rooms. Reggie remained extremely busy behind the desk and Midge carefully avoided eye contact with any tourists struggling with large cases. Almost all cases were equipped with wheels, now that porters had become a vanishing breed, and anyone who had lacked enough foresight to travel without a wheeled case deserved to struggle.

'In any case—' Victoria was saying. The word brought Midge back to attention with a guilty start. 'In any case, you'll have Roberta to help with any problems.'

'Roberta? Roberta Rinehart?'

'Yes. Haven't you heard from her? I thought she'd be here before us.'

'Not a word.' It was something new for Midge to worry about. 'No one told us she was coming.'

'Oh, I thought she'd be in touch with you herself. You have enough room, haven't you?'

'Oh yes,' Midge said. 'We can put her up in the family wing. It's quieter and she'll have more privacy there.'

'Don't count on it. Not with this lot. I've heard some of them plotting. I don't think they're going to observe any rules about places being out of bounds. I'm afraid you're going to have to lock doors.'

'We'll work something out,' Midge said vaguely, not liking to admit that most of the keys to the family wing had disappeared long ago. It had never seemed important to replace them; there were too many other necessary expenditures to be made. 'I wish someone had let me know in advance, though.'

'It's nothing to worry about,' Victoria said, promptly giving Midge another anxiety complex. 'We're both here because we want to have a little talk with you.'

'Oh,' Midge said faintly. There are few prospects more

ominous than that of having a little talk with people who hold the financial pursestrings.

'You and Reggie—' Victoria broke off as the coach driver came up to them.

'You ready?' he asked. 'I want to get on to the London road before the snow starts. I don't like the look of that sky.'

'Yes, I'm coming.' Victoria took a final look around the almost-deserted lobby, nodded, and brushed cheeks with Midge again. 'See you tomorrow night. Must dash now.' She was gone before Midge could reply.

Miss Holloway was pouring, Colonel Heather was handing round the filled cups and Lettie circulated offering plates piled high with hot buttered scones. The English tea ceremony, as mannered and timeless as the Japanese variety, was well under way. There were appreciative murmurs from the guests.

The Residents' Lounge had originally been the Morning Room and still retained the warmth and charm of its original function. Now flames leaped high and bright in the fireplace, table lamps glowed, polished wooden surfaces shone and a faint scent of potpourri hung in the air. Outside, the leaden sky grew steadily darker, as much with the oncoming storm as with the approaching night. Inside, the lounge had become a warm and sheltered oasis . . . a time capsule.

'As Treasurer of Van Dine Industries—' a short burly man had begun to play the game—'I am happy to say that we have had an excellent financial year, despite the Great Depression.'

'How lovely for you.' Miss Holloway gave him a look of blue-eyed approbation. 'One lump or two?'

'Four, if you don't mind, ma'am. They're really awfully small.'

'Quite so.' Miss Holloway plied the sugar tongs, smiling understandingly. 'You were saying, Mr . . . ?'

'Oh, yeah, sorry. I'm Stan, Stanley Marric. Er, as I was saying, I'm Treasurer of Van Dine Industries and I'm very concerned about the future of the Company. I'd hate to think that it might fall into the hands of someone who could jeopardize the market position we have gained.'

'Such a dear girl,' Miss Holloway murmured. 'I'm sure she would never do anything to upset your present excellent position . . . not knowingly.'

'Acidentally would be just as bad,' Stanley Marric said. 'It's the final result that counts—not the intention.' He stirred his tea vigorously, with the air of one who had scored an important point.

Miss Holloway smiled vaguely, allowed her gaze to rove beyond him—and blinked.

'It's all right,' one of the apparitions said gaily. 'We have that effect on everyone. You're not seeing things. There *are* two of us. We're twins.

'The Chandler twins,' the other one announced triumphantly. 'I'm Brigid and she's Lauren.' She giggled. 'Or am I Lauren and she's Brigid?'

'It doesn't matter,' the first one said. 'We always say: Call us anything, but call us!'

Miss Holloway took a deep breath. 'Two lumps or four?' she inquired sweetly.

'She's got *your* number already!' they accused each other merrily.

'Those girls have been the life of the party,' a tall, gaunt man confided to Colonel Heather. 'I'm Dixon Carr, by the way.' He was wearing a blood-red name tag with DIXON in black Gothic lettering. 'My friends call me Dix.'

Colonel Heather nodded and managed to slide away without divulging his own name, rank and serial number. For a moment, it appeared that Dix might be about to follow his new-found friend, but a new arrival in the doorway distracted everyone.

Evelina T. Carterslee stood there, carefully surveying the lounge before venturing inside. A murmur of recognition rose from several groups. She moved forward smiling and, first things first, made straight for the tea-trolley.

Miss Holloway had the tea poured to her liking and ready for her as she reached the trolley. 'A goodly turnout,' Miss Holloway murmured, handing Evelina her cup. There were always some who remained in their rooms, unpacking or resting, until the Welcoming Cocktail Party. A few extreme cases could be counted on to skip tea, deeming it more important to roam the corridors and establish the lie of the land before the action started.

'Indeed,' Evelina murmured back. 'Where is dear Victoria?' She took a proprietory interest in everything about The Crimson Shroud Bookshop, since it had been named after her first novel.

'I believe she went back to London for the night. She'll be down tomorrow for the rest of the weekend.'

'I see.' Evelina did not look pleased. 'Then I must assume that I am on duty now and it will be up to me to act as hostess for the tour.'

'That's right,' Grace said heartlessly. 'Start circulating. You're part of the entertainment.'

Several spectators remarked among themselves on the cold look Evelina turned on Grace before walking over to the nearest group and forcing a smile.

'Is anything wrong?' one of them asked eagerly.

'Not to my knowledge,' Evelina said. 'Are you one of the Van Dine shareholders or one of the executives?'

There were flustered glances exchanged. Evelina waited patiently, sipping her tea.

'I'm the Personnel Manager of Van Dine Industries,' a short heavily-built woman said, unsmiling. 'My name is Bertha Stout—and I'd rather not have any cracks about it.'

'A very responsible position,' Evelina said smoothly. 'I'm delighted to have the opportunity to meet you. As one of the major shareholders in Van Dine Industries, I've welcomed the opportunity to meet so many of the marvellous people who have done so much to keep the company on an even keel during these difficult times.'

'I'm Haila Bond,' a small wiry terrier of a female announced. 'I'm a major shareholder, too.'

'No, you're not.' Someone contradicted her. 'You said you were going to be a Sales Executive.'

'Well, I've changed my mind,' Haila said firmly. 'There are too many Sales Executives already.'

Evelina took another sip of tea, waiting until they sorted out their stories.

'I don't care,' the sole man in the group declared. 'I'm Asey Wentworth and I'm Group Sales Director.'

'Then you can take a great deal of credit for the excellent results last year.' Evelina beamed approval at him.

'That's right. And I always say—' He gave Haila Bond a dirty look. 'I always say there can never be too many Sales Executives.'

'Quite right.' Someone else had edged into the group. 'I'm a Sales Executive—and proud of it. I've taken the Top Salesman Award three years running. That's why my wife and I have been given this free trip to England—as an extra prize. I'm Norman Dain and this is my wife, Alice.'

'I'm so pleased and thrilled to meet you,' Alice gushed. 'I hope you'll let me have your autograph before this weekend is over. Oh dear—' A frown from her husband got through to her. 'Have I said something wrong? Shouldn't I admit I know your name? Are . . . are you one of the Van Dines?'

'It's quite all right, my dear,' Evelina purred. 'I *am* Evelina T. Carterslee and I have invested some of my royalties in Van Dine Industries. That's why I'm here, but I *am* myself.'

'Oh, thank goodness,' Alice said. 'I have a feeling this weekend is going to get awfully confused. The Chandler twins have shouted at me already because I forgot they were supposed to be Private Secretaries to old Ellery Van Dine and had been left a share of the business in a codicil to his Will.'

'Alice—' her husband warned.

'I don't care. I told them I didn't think we were starting properly until the cocktail party. Now, tell me, are we?'

'Well . . .' Evelina temporized. 'I think everyone must work themselves into their roles at their own pace. Whatever is easier for you.'

'That's it,' Bertha Stout approved. 'The game's always afoot, eh?'

'Well . . .' Evelina said again, stealing a quick glance at her watch. 'Almost always.'

There was a scream of brakes from the carriageway outside.

'Something's happening!' the Chandler twins shrieked in unison and led the dash to the lobby.

An open sports car had drawn up outside the front entrance. Two young men leaped out and began removing luggage from the boot. One, sedately dressed in business suit with waistcoat, had a matched set of leather cases; the other, in plus-fours and tweed jacket, had two unmatched, rather cheap-looking cases.

They left their cases piled beside the car and advanced up the stone steps.

'They're coming! They're coming!' the Chandler twins squealed.

'Who are they? . . . Who are they?' The others crowded into the lobby, leaving a respectable space for events to play themselves out. 'Are they part of it?' They fell back still further as the door opened.

As they entered, the young man in the business suit threw his arms about the other's shoulder and they laughed exaggeratedly at a joke that had obviously just been made.

'Good afternoon.' Reggie moved forward to greet them, raising his voice so that those at the back could hear. 'You must be Mr Edwin Lupin,' he said to the man in the business suit. 'We've been expecting you, sir. But I'm afraid . . . ?' He looked askance at the man accompanying him.

'An old friend of mine I ran into in London,' Edwin Lupin

said easily. 'I invited him along for the weekend. I'm sure Sir Cedric won't mind.'

'ALGIE!' The Honourable Petronella appeared at the head of the staircase and raced down it to throw herself into the other man's arms.

'Oh, Algie, darling! You've found me! I knew you wouldn't leave me to moulder in this rotten place! Darling, darling, Algie! We're together once more—and no one will ever be able to part us again!'

CHAPTER 7

'Did you see the way she looked at him? She's besotted, all right. And him! That terrible little thin moustache—he even *looks* like a cad. If he ever gets his hands on her money, she won't keep it for ten minutes. They'll run Van Dine Industries right down into the ground.'

'But what was Edwin doing bringing that man along? Surely he must have known . . .'

'Of course he did. He's deliberately trying to ruin Petronella's chances. Keep your eye on him. He may look as though butter wouldn't melt in his mouth, but I wouldn't trust him as far as I could throw him.'

The discussion was as spirited as the drinks at the Welcoming Cocktail Party. Those who had been present at the arrival of Edwin and Algie were discussing it and filling-in the guests who had missed it.

They were all wearing their blood-red name tags with the black Gothic lettering now, Midge observed. That would make it easier to identify, if not keep track of them. Already, some were showing an alarming tendency to wander farther afield than other tours had done. Once the 'secret passage'— the servants' staircase—had been disclosed to them, as it must be, there would be no way of keeping track of their whereabouts.

Reggie was being kept busy behind the bar. He had pre-mixed shakers full of the most colourful cocktails and the Art Deco cocktail glasses stood waiting, filled with the bright blue of Blue Train, the clear red of Luigi and the green of Shamrock, giving an extra-festive air to the proceedings.

Midge deftly and inconspicuously refilled the little saucers with salted almonds and peanuts and the larger bowls with potato crisps. Not that it would have attracted any attention if she had done it after a fanfare of trumpets. The guests were becoming too deeply immersed in their role-playing to notice.

Some guests were drifting back to the bar for refills now. After dinner, the cash bar would be in operation and they were making the most of the complimentary cocktails. Making too much of them, perhaps. The snare and delusion of the cocktails was that they were so sweet that the strength of them might pass unnoticed until it was too late. Midge's forehead furrowed as she saw that several were switching drinks to try another colour which had caught their fancy. Oh well, the recipe for the Prairie Oyster was looming large above them. On their heads be it.

'Oh, look! Who are they?' There was a stir as two strangers entered the bar. Several guests smiled tentatively at them. There was a rustle of expectancy, as at a curtain about to rise.

'Good evening, everyone,' Cedric said. 'May I officially welcome you to Chortlesby Manor? I am Sir Cedric Strangeways—and this is my, er . . . sister, Lady Hermione Marsh—'

It wasn't quite accurate, but the guests were lapping it up along with the cocktails. Cedric and Hermione had insisted on having titles, allowing art to make up for what nature had denied them. To Hermione's initial chagrin, the first tour had got her title wrong, preferring the matey 'Lady Hermione' to the official 'Lady Marsh'. Had she kept correcting them, they would have assumed that she was stuffy and stand-offish and it would have diminished their enjoyment. In deference to their trans-Atlantic sensibilities, Lady Hermione she remained. It had to be admitted that this also made the switch to first names after the solution much simpler.

Lady Hermione accepted a Blue Train from Reggie and began to circulate, smiling graciously at the guests. Only when the subject of the Honourable Petronella was raised, did her smile frost over.

'She'll be down later,' Lady Hermione told Stanley Marric, Treasurer of Van Dine Industries. 'She has . . . been delayed . . .'

'She's not with that man, is she?' Stan asked suspiciously.

Lady Hermione lifted an eyebrow. 'What man?'

'That's right,' someone stage-whispered. 'She wasn't here at tea. Maybe she doesn't know yet.'

'I think Sir Cedric should throw him out. He's nothing but a gate-crasher.'

'Still, it's better we get a good look at him so that we can make the right decision, isn't it?'

'With any luck, maybe somebody will murder him before the weekend is over!' There was a gust of conspiratorial laughter at this suggestion.

'They promised us Bramwell Barbour was going to be here—' The Chandler twins were more interested in the missing celebrity than in the game. 'Where is he? Did he cancel out? Maybe we can get our money back.'

'No, no, my dear young ladies—' Unfortunately, they had made their complaint to Cedric, the weakest link in the chain. He showed faint signs of panic. 'He's here. He'll be down shortly, I'm sure. Unless, of course, he's tied up with his new book. He's working hard, you know. Very hard—'

'They *promised* . . .' One indistinguishable twin appeared on the verge of tears, the other was beginning to look belligerent. 'We wouldn't have come, otherwise.'

'Oh, I'm sure he'll put in an appearance—'

'An appearance!' That wasn't good enough. 'He'd better do more than that. They said he'd be with us *all weekend*.'

'Yes, yes.' Cedric began backing away. 'And I'm sure he will be. Work schedule permitting—'

'Would anyone like another drink?' Midge moved in to rescue Cedric before he met an untimely fate. The twins looked ready to murder him and, although he was due for the chop, it was not supposed to happen until after dinner. He had several plot lines to deliver first— if he remembered them.

Sir Cedric was going to be the first victim simply because he was so bad at delivering his lines. It had seemed the simplest solution for one who desperately wanted to be part of the action but was too self-conscious to throw himself into it utterly.

'I don't want another drink, I want Bramwell Barbour.' The speaker's name tag said that she was Lauren, but Midge did not necessarily believe that. She suspected that the twins thought it the height of wit to exchange their name tags, possibly several times in one evening.

'Try whistling!' Brigid said and screamed with hysterical laughter.

'Who are you?' Lauren ignored her twin and frowned at Midge. 'Where do you come into this?'

'I'm Reggie's wife; I'm housekeeper and Reggie is butler to Sir Cedric Strangeways.' Midge went into her cover story. 'Sir Cedric offered us employment after Reggie had to leave his post at New Scotland Yard because of ill-health.'

'Ill-health, eh?' Bertha Stout had come up behind them and was shamelessly eavesdropping. 'He looks all right to me. What's the matter with him?'

'He's a lot better now,' Midge said. 'This country air has done him a world of good. We're terribly grateful to Sir Cedric.'

'She didn't answer.' Haila Bond closed in on the group, her eyes snapping. 'Make her answer the question. What's wrong with Reggie?'

'Nothing serious, really.' Midge shrugged. 'Just a slight heart murmur. It doesn't bother him at all.'

'But it bothered Scotland Yard enough to dismiss him.' They turned and studied Reggie speculatively, measuring his chances as prospective victim—or possibly, about-to-be-murderer.

'He wasn't dismissed,' Midge said loyally. 'He was invalided out. But the pension—the part-pension—was so small . . . Besides, he's much too young a man to hang about doing nothing.'

Cedric had taken the opportunity to slip away while Midge was under fire. He strolled over to have a quiet word with Grace Holloway, watched by several pairs of intent eyes. He was doing quite well but, inevitably, he would begin to twitch before the end of the evening. Fortunately, that could be put down to oncoming symptoms.

'Lady Hermione—' Edwin Lupin entered and made his way unerringly to his hostess. 'How kind of you to have us all here. It's very sporting of you.'

'It's the least I could do—' Lady Hermione swept him with a remote, contemptuous look—'for dear Petronella.' She swept another look over him and ostentatiously turned away. Definitely, she would require a lorgnette if they were to use this script for other weekends.

'Nuts?' Lettie, wearing a fetchingly abbreviated maid's costume with crisp white apron and cap, pushed her serving tray at Edwin. He ogled her briefly, then allowed his face to become a smooth mask.

'No, thanks,' he said and turned away.

'He likes her,' someone hazarded.

'No, he doesn't. He hates her. I'll bet he knows her. They've met before.'

Speculation began to build. Lettie, unsmiling, bore down on the most vociferous group. They silenced at her approach. Meekly, they helped themselves to the hot cocktail sausages and sandwiches on her tray.

'Mmm, this is good.' Alice Dain bit into the tiny triangular sandwich. 'What is it? I can't quite place—'

'Chopped toasted almonds,' Lettie answered, poker-faced. 'The bread is spread with mayonnaise.'

'Very tasty,' Norman Dain approved, disposing of his in one gulp.

'There's a lot of almonds around here tonight,' Dixon Carr commented. 'What's the betting on cyanide and that famous bitter almonds smell?'

Lettie moved away, refusing to comprehend the joke convulsing the group.

'Hey, we didn't ask her any questions,' someone realized.

'Time enough, time enough,' Dix said. 'We're just getting started. Wait until things warm up.'

'Here comes a heatwave now.' Norman gestured to the entrance.

The Honourable Petronella stood there, clinging shamelessly to the arm of Algernon Moriarty. They posed there long enough to allow the guests to come to the gradual realization that another scene was about to start. Silence fell, all eyes turned to the couple.

'You!' Realization struck Lady Hermione belatedly. She had been talking to Colonel Heather, now she charged forward, eyes blazing. 'What are you doing here? Who let you in? I gave orders—'

'He came down with me, Lady Hermione—' Nobly, Edwin Lupin stepped forward to divert her wrath. 'I invited him. He's my guest.'

'He's my guest, too,' the Hon. Pet declared defiantly.

'How dare you?' Lady Hermione turned the full force of her rage on Algie. 'You know you're not welcome here!'

'Oh, I say,' he protested, wincing. 'I've had two invitations. You heard 'em. I mean, two against one . . .' He faltered into silence under her furious glare.

'Something the matter here?' Sir Cedric doddered forward vaguely. 'Something upsetting you, Hermione?'

'Oh, Uncle Cedric—' The Hon. Pet relinquished Algie's arm briefly to hurl herself at Sir Cedric. 'Aunt Hermione is just being nasty because she didn't invite Algie herself. But Edwin did, and I want him to stay, too. You don't mind, do you?' She tweaked his ear. 'You will let him stay, won't you? Say you will—please, please, please!'

'Anything you like, my dear.' Sir Cedric patted her fondly. 'Friend of yours, eh what?'

'Oh yes, Uncle Cedric. Thank you, thank you, thank—'

'Cedric,' Lady Hermione said chillingly, 'I want to speak to you! In private!' She led him from the room.

'Don't go,' someone called out irreverently. 'You'll be sorry!'

'Hoo, boy, is he gonna get it!' someone else said.

A small party detached themselves from the others and stalked after Sir Cedric and Lady Hermione. They had placed their bets on the main suspects and they were going to shadow them in the hope of discovering something incriminating.

'There, that's settled—' The Hon. Pet flashed them all a brilliant smile. 'Now, Algie, darling, get me a drink!'

Algie sketched a salute and departed in the direction of the bar. Lettie moved over and offered Petronella her tray. The Hon. Pet looked, hesitated, then caught up one of the toasted almond triangles.

'I simply adore these,' she cooed. She bit daintily and munched while an interested audience waited to see whether or not she was going to drop dead on the spot.

'Delicious,' she said, and took two more. Most of her audience watched avidly, although a couple of restless ones had begun to drift away, rightly suspecting that there were more red herrings than almonds in the sandwiches.

'*There* he is!' Midge was close enough to hear the triumphant whisper of one Chandler twin to the other. She followed the direction of their combined gaze.

Bramwell Barbour was sidling into the bar, obviously trying to be inconspicuous. He was failing dismally.

'*Does your mother know you're out . . . ?*' Lettie hummed softly, giving her short skirt an extra swish.

'Bramwell! . . . Oh, Bram!' The Chandler twins closed in on him in a pincers movement.

'Oh!' Bramwell Barbour flinched visibly as the twins bore down on him. Only by an effort of will—made against his better judgement—did he appear to stand his ground.

'Bram! Bram!' they cried. 'Surprise!'

'Er, yes. Yes, it certainly is. What are you two doing here? I mean, I never expected . . . I thought . . .'

'Oh, you know us,' Brigid, or perhaps it was Lauren, giggled. 'We just can't tear ourselves away from you.'

'Where's Amaryllis?' the other one asked, on a note of dawning hope. 'Didn't she come over with you.?'

'Oh yes, yes, she's here.' He looked around wildly, but Amaryllis was not in sight. His gaze lighted on Midge.

'Where is she?' he demanded frantically. 'Where's my mother?'

'Mother?' Dixon Carr's face went blank with astonishment. He turned to Lettie, who was gripping her tray so savagely that her knuckles were turning white. '*That's* Bramwell Barbour? The one who writes all those tough sexy books? You mean he travels with his *mother*?'

'Incredible, isn't it?' Lettie spoke between clenched teeth. 'He's utterly under her thumb. It's a wonder he dared move out of his room without her permission.'

'Amaryllis took the car into Salisbury.' Midge spoke quickly and loudly, trying to drown out the conversation going on beside her. 'She left well before tea. I thought she'd have returned by now, but I've been too busy to check on it. Hasn't she come back?'

'She can't have.' For once, Bramwell spoke decisively. 'I haven't seen her.'

'Oh.' That was fairly conclusive. If Amaryllis had not been seen recently by her son, it was because she was not in the vicinity. It was unthinkable that she should be anywhere within the confines of Chortlesby Manor and not have come down to meet the tour with Bramwell. Also, he would never have been allowed to wear that tie if his mother had seen it first.

'Then where is she?' Bramwell seemed on the verge of panic. 'What's happened to her?'

'I'm sure she won't be long.' Midge tried to soothe him. 'Perhaps she ran out of petrol or had a flat tyre.'

'Then why didn't she call me? She should have let me know.'

'This is incredible,' Dix murmured to Lettie. 'I just can't believe it. All those macho books . . .'

'Don't worry—' Brigid said.

'Never mind—' Lauren said.

'You've still got us!' they chorused.

'But I don't wa—' He stopped himself just in time. 'I want my—' He stopped again.

'Unbelievable.' Dix shook his head. 'It just goes to show, you can't judge an author by his books.'

'You certainly can't,' Lettie snarled.

'Tell me,' Dix said carefully. 'What is his mother like?'

'I could be sued,' Lettie said, 'if anyone heard me giving a true description of that man-eating sow!'

'Please!' Dix winced, holding up his hands.

'Wait until you see her!'

'But if she hasn't come back, perhaps there's something wrong. Maybe she's met with an accident . . . a serious accident.'

'Not her,' Lettie sighed. 'No such luck. That old battleaxe is too tough to die.'

CHAPTER 8

The first course at dinner was greatly appreciated—and in the right manner. These guests were alert to every nuance.

'Mushroom soup, eh?' Dix kept a properly straight face. 'I hope you were pretty careful about getting the right mushrooms.'

'It was no trouble at all.' Midge briskly ladled soup from

the steaming tureen. 'Sir Cedric gathered them himself this morning.'

'Sir Cedric? Isn't he the absent-minded one?'

'He's just a little vague,' Midge said encouragingly.

'Oh boy! And you let *him* pick the mushrooms?' Norman Dain leaned over his bowl and sniffed at the fragrant cloud arising from it. 'We'd better watch our step.'

There was a gust of nervous laughter. They watched each other and tried to pretend that they were not keeping a close watch on the prospective victim seated at their table.

The tables had been arranged so that one actor or accomplice was seated at each table, in order to feed plot lines in the guise of gossip and snippets of information which might be useful or might be red herrings. It was the task of the guests to sort out the wheat from the chaff and try to retain the proper clues which would be needed later. They hung on every word and asked leading questions, although they could have no idea of what they should be asking until after the victim had been killed.

Everyone had now tasted their soup and there had been no dramatic developments. They relaxed into cautious enjoyment of the soup. Obviously, nothing was going to happen during this course.

'Of course, it takes a while,' someone pointed out. 'Mushrooms aren't instantaneous—like some other poisons we could all mention.'

'Please don't,' Bramwell Barbour said grimly, with the air of one who had enough problems. As, indeed, he had.

He was seated between the Chandler twins, which Midge found most interesting as she had personally placed him at a table on the other side of the room. The twins were obviously as adept at switching place cards as at exchanging identification tags. She made a mental note to check the seating arrangements before the guests filed into the dining-room for future meals.

That didn't help poor Bram tonight, however. He hunched over his bowl of soup, spooning it up rapidly, his hunted expression growing as the twins giggled and nudged him, delighted with themselves and the prize they had captured.

Midge hoped that he wouldn't seek escape by collapsing and pretending that *he* was the intended victim. That would throw everything out of kilter, but he was looking desperate enough for anything.

Fortunately, the first course was finished quickly and the main course provided distraction aplenty. Fish and Chips, served rolled up in copies of the *Daily Mirror* for various dates in November 1934. They read out snippets to each other:

'Hey, DEATH OF "ALICE" OF WONDERLAND—Lewis Carroll's "Ideal Child" Dies at 82 . . .'

'How about November 20th: HALF ENGLAND UNDER FOG PALL—A hundred thousand people besieged London and suburban railway stations last night struggling to get home from business . . .'

'And look at this for a double feature—remember them? William Powell and Myrna Loy in *The Thin Man* and Ginger Rogers and Dick Powell in *Twenty Million Sweethearts*.'

'And you could get a Ford car for £115 plus £6 tax!'

'Don't forget there was five dollars to the pound then.'

'Even so—and here's a coat at Swan and Edgar's for seventy-five shillings—with a "real Skunk" collar!'

The distraction carried them through to dessert. They studied the dish set before them as a promise of things to come.

'Almonds again!' Dix squinted at the toasted almond flakes sprinkled over the Amaretto-laced vanilla ice-cream. 'I tell you, they're out to get us!'

'They're out to get somebody.' Haila Bond's beady little eyes gleamed, she looked around the table avidly.

'My favourite sweet!' Miss Holloway took a spoonful of the ice-cream, raised it to her lips and—tantalizingly—lowered it again to speak over her shoulder to Midge. 'But you usually serve those nice little almond macaroons with it.' The reminder should have come from Cedric, but he was deep in conversation with Alice Dain.

'I'll bring some right away,' Midge said. Keeping a straight face, she hurried off. It was marvellous the way Miss Holloway was playing more of a role with every tour. Most of them were certain she was one of the actors, whereas few people realized until quite late in the game that Lettie wasn't a real maid. In fact, on the last tour, one hopeful gentleman had remained unconvinced to the end and had earnestly entreated Lettie to give up this dead-end job and return to the States with him and let him look after her, if not actually marry her. Had she really been a maid, Lettie had admitted, the offer might have been quite tempting.

Lettie was in the kitchen, loading a tray with demi-tasse cups. 'For this I got my Equity card!' she said.

'You're perfect in the role.' Midge took time out to stroke an edgy ego. 'As usual, no one suspects you're part of the act. When you start screaming, they'll believe you.'

'I'd like to do more than scream!' Lettie's face darkened. 'I'd like to pour boiling oil—or at least coffee—over those two harpies molesting Bram!'

'Better not,' Midge advised. 'They're too far apart. You could only get one of them—and you wouldn't know which one to choose.'

'That's true, they're equally awful. Oh well,' Lettie sighed. 'I'll just have to wait until Amaryllis gets back. For once, it will be a pleasure to see her in action. She'll make short work of those two.'

'I hope she's all right.' Midge spared a moment for another worry. 'I mean, I hope there hasn't been an accident. We need the car.'

'Amaryllis we can do without,' Lettie agreed. 'It isn't like her to miss a meal, but perhaps she decided to eat in town this once. She was complaining about fish and chips being on the menu again.'

'The guests love them. It's what they expect in England

and—' Midge raised her voice to take in another hovering ego—'Cook does them to perfection.'

'If against the odds,' Cook said sharply. 'I had to let the help go home early. The snow's started and they were afraid they wouldn't make it if they didn't leave before time.'

'Oh dear. I've been so busy I hadn't noticed.' Midge glanced towards the window over the sink. Outside, large fluttering white flakes could be seen against the black sky in the light shining out from the kitchen. 'I hope they won't have any trouble getting back in the morning.'

'It probably won't last long.' Lettie picked up her tray and headed for the door. 'But wouldn't it be lovely if it was just bad enough to maroon Sweet Amaryllis in town all night?'

'Bramwell might not think so,' Midge reminded her. 'I'm sure he's counting on his mother to take care of the terrible twins for him. I suspect she's had plenty of experience with them, they all seem to know each other of old.'

Ackroyd had been sitting looking from one speaker to the other, now he rose and strolled nonchalantly towards the door.

'Oh no you don't.' Midge blocked his way with her foot. 'You know you're not allowed in the dining-room.'

Ackroyd turned his back on her, sat down, and became very busy washing his white ruff and shirtfront.

'It's obvious they've chased him all the way over here—' Lettie braced her tray and swung her hip against the door. 'And it's not fair. It's two to one and he's so gormless they might actually catch him. Come back, Amaryllis, all is forgiven—for the moment.'

Raised voices could be heard in the dining-room just before the door swung shut behind Lettie. Midge glanced at her watch and nodded. Right on schedule. A nice little row was due to keep the pot bubbling for the amateur sleuths until the party adjourned to the drawing-room for coffee and liqueurs. She caught up a plate of macaroons and returned to the dining-room to referee.

'I don't care—' The Honourable Petronella was on her feet blazing defiance at Lady Hermione. 'It's stupid, it's petty, it's—it's *archaic*! This is 1935! You can't force the women to leave the room so that the men can linger over their port.'

'It is the custom,' Lady Hermione said coldly. 'It has always been done.'

'Then it's time it stopped! *You* don't want to leave the room, do you?' Throwing her arms wide, Petronella appealed to the other women. 'Why don't we stay here and help ourselves to the port, too? They can't throw us out bodily!'

'Oh . . . um . . .' Thus appealed to, the females of the Murder at the Manor Tour looked to each other for support, possibly a lead. They weren't sure which way they were supposed to respond.

'Come now, Pet—' Sir Cedric pushed back his chair. 'You've had your way once today. Let it go at that, eh?' He forced a smile, glancing around, and tried a feeble joke. 'We mere males ought to have a few minutes to ourselves now and again. We might have things to discuss. For instance, I might want to ask your young man his intentions.'

'His intentions are perfectly clear,' Lady Hermione informed her brother. 'He intends to get his hands on Petronella's money and spend it as fast as he's able— before she comes to her senses and throws him out!'

'Oh, I say,' Sir Cedric protested. 'Have a care. After all, the chap *is* a guest under my roof.'

'And whose fault is that, you fool?' Lady Hermione turned on him like a striking cobra. 'If you'd had one grain of sense—' Belatedly, she seemed to remember her enthralled audience.

'Oh, you're hopeless!' She turned and swept from the room.

'Oh no!' Petronella rushed after her. 'You come back here and apologize to Algie!'

There was a momentary silence in the wake of their

departure. Then Miss Holloway rose to her feet.

'*Hhrrk-hhrrk* . . .' She had been practising her dry cough. It drew all eyes to her. 'I believe—' she smiled into the expectant faces. 'I believe we should follow the lead of our hostess. Ladies, shall we adjourn to the Withdrawing-Room?'

The fire in the drawing-room was blazing brightly. Three card tables had been set up for bridge. On another table a Mah Jong set spilled its gleaming mysteries across green baize. In the background Jack Buchanan crooned beguilingly from the gramophone.

'Oh, it's perfect!' Alice Dain gave a shiver of delight. 'It's just the way I always imagined a country house would be.'

'And there's a storm outside—' Bertha Stout let the velvet drape fall back into place, her voice dripping with relish. 'A real blizzard. We'll be cut off from all human contact by morning.'

'No! . . . Really? . . . Let's see . . .' Several of them rushed to the windows to confirm the weather prediction.

'We're not cut off yet—' One of the twins turned away from the window and registered a complaint. 'There's a car coming up the drive.'

'Ooh! What now?' There was a rush from windows to the lobby. 'Who is it?'

'I suppose—' Evelina T. Carterslee seated herself behind the coffee table piled with waiting demi-tasse cups. 'I suppose it's Amaryllis.' She sighed. 'The peace was too good to last.'

With a sinking heart, Midge silently agreed with Evelina's deduction. It had been too much to hope for, that Amaryllis would let anything so minor as a blizzard keep her from Bramwell's side. Just in case, however, Midge joined the others in the lobby to see who was going to come through the front door.

Amaryllis, of course. How could she have doubted it?

But another figure loomed immediately behind Amaryllis.

'Roberta!' Midge stepped forward to welcome the proprietor of the Death On Wheels Bookshop. 'Victoria said you were coming. You should have let us know.'

'*I* knew,' Amaryllis said. 'I collected her at the station. We had dinner in town.'

'You're just in time to join us for coffee and liqueurs.' Midge ignored Amaryllis's rudeness, she was so accustomed to it by now that only the lack of it would have surprised her. 'Let Reggie bring your things in from the car and come into the drawing-room.'

'Where's Bramwell?' Amaryllis was already in the doorway and surveying the room.

'The gentlemen are lingering over their port,' Midge said. 'They'll be with us shortly.'

'I'll take my coat upstairs first, then.' Amaryllis paused. 'Shall I take yours, Roberta?'

'No, that's all right.' Roberta Rinehart was huddled into a plaid wool car coat. 'I'll keep it on for a while.' She sent Midge a wan smile. 'I'm not acclimatized to English temperatures yet—especially the indoor ones.'

'A drink will warm you up.' Midge led the way into the drawing-room. The tour members, sensing a false alarm, had already retreated inside and were queueing for their coffee.

'It's only *her*,' Midge heard one Chandler twin report to the other, making the sort of face Amaryllis inevitably seemed to inspire.

'Oh, pooh!' According to her name tag, it was Lauren who returned the grimace, but Midge had noticed that the twin with the congealing spot of sticky ice-cream on her bodice had been labelled Brigid when she left the table. They had obviously changed name tags again, unaware that they were now distinguishable—at least for the remainder of the evening. What a shame that they'd be wearing different clothes tomorrow.

Although the tour greeted her enthusiastically enough,

Roberta's arrival was upstaged by the return of Lady Hermione and the Honourable Petronella, now apparently back on the best of terms.

Evelina continued to deal out the demi-tasses. 'Black or white?' she asked Roberta.

'Nothing for me, thanks. I'd never be able to sleep.' Roberta did not look as though she had been sleeping well for some time.

'Let me get you a brandy instead,' Midge said. 'That won't keep you awake.'

'Just a small one,' Roberta said. 'I'm really so exhausted I think I'll slip away as soon as—'

'Whelp! Insolent young pup!' Doors slammed. Sir Cedric stormed into the drawing-room, followed by the males of the tour in varying stages of consternation.

'You were right, damn it!' Sir Cedric made directly for Lady Hermione. 'He's a scoundrel! A cad! Do you know what he just said to me?'

'What did he say?' Hermione watched Cedric carefully, ready to prompt if he should forget his lines.

'Told me the Light Brigade should have disobeyed orders!' Cedric was well into his part, as indignant as though he really were a military historian. 'Not only that, but he said most of the commanders in the Great War were incompetent morons. He said—' Sir Cedric choked. 'He said that if war were to be declared right now, he, for one, wouldn't fight!'

'I told you so!' Lady Hermione said triumphantly. 'The man's an absolute rotter!'

'See here, Sir Cedric, you mustn't let him upset you like this.' Dix was earnestly trying to pour oil on the troubled waters. 'Lots of the youngsters are going around saying things like that these days. They don't mean it. Why, when the war breaks out—I mean, if war comes, they'll be the first ones to join up and fight. You'll see.'

'Not him!' Sir Cedric snarled. 'He meant every word of it. The man's a lily-livered coward!'

'How can you say that?' Petronella cried. 'He wasn't afraid to speak his mind to you, was he?'

'Here, Sir Cedric—' Lettie was at his side, proffering a cup. 'Here's your coffee—just the way you like it.'

'Eh?' Sir Cedric took the cup and glanced down at it absently. 'Thank you. You're a good girl, Lettie.'

'The gentleman is quite right, Cedric,' Lady Hermione said. 'You mustn't let yourself get so excited. It isn't good for you. Sit down and let's have a few rubbers of bridge.'

'Do you want me to be calm or do you want me to play bridge with you?' Cedric asked. 'You can't have it both ways.'

Lady Hermione threw him a quelling look. He was adlibbing; that wasn't in the script. Nor was Sir Cedric supposed to have a sense of humour.

'Cedric—' She sat at one of the bridge tables and gestured him to the chair opposite her. 'Petronella—Edwin—Come and make up the table.'

Edwin moved forward obediently, but Petronella looked rebellious.

'Come along, Sweet Coz.' Edwin took her elbow and led her to the table. 'We ought to get to know each other better. We have so much in common.'

'Bramwell, come and partner me!' Evelina plucked her grateful colleague from the toils of the Chandler twins as neatly as his mother could have done. She then forestalled their concerted move to make up the table by moving to the table already occupied by Alice and Norman Dain. 'May we join you?' she asked.

'Please do.' Norman leaped to his feet, jarring the table and sending the cards sliding. 'We'd be honoured.'

Reggie and Midge moved from table to table and group to group, serving brandy and liqueurs. Most of the guests were now milling about, apparently aimlessly, but never moving far out of sight of the bridge table at which the principal actors were now seated. A few of them were keeping a close watch on Algie, who had thrown himself into an armchair and buried his face in the January 1935 issue of *Country Life*.

Sir Cedric sipped alternately at his coffee and his brandy as Lady Hermione shuffled the cards. The small sound as she slapped them down in front of Petronella to cut was clearly audible. Petronella cut automatically, Lady Hermione gathered up the cards, shuffled them again, and began to deal.

This was the signal for some of the more eager to drift over and stand behind the chairs of the players, prepared to give advice.

Everyone except Sir Cedric picked up the hand dealt and fanned out the cards for a preliminary assessment. Sir Cedric sat slumped in his chair, staring blankly at the cards face down on the table before him.

'I say, Hermione,' he said plaintively. 'I—I—' He broke off, looking around wildly.

Midge moved into his range of vision, standing just behind the onlookers and mouthed his next line at him. His face cleared slightly as he followed her lips.

'I—' He ran his hand across his forehead. 'I feel deucedly peculiar—'

'I've told you before—' Lady Hermione began.

'Aaaagh—' Sir Cedric lurched to his feet, overturning his chair. The onlookers behind him moved back sharply.

'Aaaargh . . .' He clutched at his throat and pitched forward full length on the floor.

From the doorway, Lettie began screaming.

'. . . et . . .' Sir Cedric raised his head weakly, his hand stretched out imploringly in her direction. '. . . et . . .' The word died in his throat. His body went limp, his head fell back to the carpet with a dull thud.

Lettie went on screaming.

CHAPTER 9

'Someone give me a hand.' Reggie dashed to the side of the fallen Sir Cedric. 'Help me get him to his room.'

'He's dead!' The Chandler twins began screaming also. 'He's dead! He's dead! He's been murdered!'

'Nonsense!' Lady Hermione flashed a look of pure venom at them. 'The old fool has forgotten his pills again. And he knows I hate playing with a dummy. Stop that noise, girl!' She turned her venom on Lettie.

'Take his feet,' Reggie ordered Edwin, who had rushed to help. They took a careful grip on Cedric, lifted him from the floor and headed for the doorway, staggering under his dead weight.

'What happened? What happened?' Those who had mounted guard over Algie abandoned him and surged over to the bridge table which had been the scene of the action.

'He said he wasn't feeling well—right after a gulp of that coffee.'

'Naw, he said he was feeling peculiar—and it was just after he drank some brandy.

'Is anyone—' Lady Hermione asked coldly. 'Is anyone going to pick up Cedric's hand and give me a game of bridge?'

'How can you be so cold, so unfeeling?' Petronella threw down her own hand and glared at Lady Hermione. 'Your own brother carried out—perhaps dead—and all you can think of is bridge!'

Lettie, hands over her face and sobbing wildly, had been led to a sofa and settled into it by several of the guests.

'Stand back. Give her air,' someone instructed.

'Here.' Dix pushed forward carrying a glass and bent over Lettie solicitously. 'Have a brandy. That's what you need.'

'Oh, thank you, sir.' Lettie groped blindly for the glass,

found it and took a deep gulp. Immediately, she coughed and spluttered. Dix had gone behind the bar himself in Reggie's absence and she had been given a straight cognac rather than the cold tea she had expected.

'You're callous! Unfeeling!' Petronella shrieked. 'I can't stand you!' She stumbled away from the table.

'Steady on, old girl.' Algie crossed to her and put an arm around her shoulders. 'Steady, Pet.' He assisted her out of the room.

'Well—!' Lady Hermione threw down her hand. 'If no one is going to play—!' She stood up and stalked from the room.

Stanley Marric bent over the table and examined her discarded cards. 'No wonder she's so mad,' he said. 'She had a great hand here.'

'How can you think of a thing like that at a time like this?' Haila Bond snapped. 'You're as bad as she is.'

'Bram—' The Chandler twins moved over to flank their prey. 'Bram, aren't you going to do something? Sir Cedric has just been murdered. Aren't you going to solve the case?'

'No,' Bram said. Unnerved, he led with the wrong card and lost the trick.

'We don't know that it was murder,' Evelina pointed out loudly. 'We're not even sure that Sir Cedric is dead. All we know at this point is that he was indisposed and has been taken to his room.'

'Is that going to be your story?' Until Sir Cedric's collapse, Bertha Stout had been sitting at the Mah Jong table, moodily examining the gleaming mother-of-pearl counters and speculating with the other people at the table as to the possible rules of the game. (Unfortunately, the set Reggie had unearthed at a local antique shop had not included a copy of the rules and no one had any idea of how the game should be played. It was there for decorative purposes— and as a genuine period touch.)

'You're not going to help, either?' Bertha Stout challenged Evelina. 'There are going to be no flashes of insight from the brilliant mind that created Luigi von Murphy?'

'Not at the moment.' Evelina calmly led a trump, to the consternation of Alice Dain.

'Then—' Bertha Stout looked round at the others and uttered the rallying cry they had all been waiting for. 'Then we'll have to solve it ourselves!'

'Oh, how can you? How can you?' Lettie leaped to her feet, glaring at them accusingly. 'Poor Cedric's not even cold yet—and you're treating it like some sort of game!' She turned and rushed from the room.

'Aha,' Dix said thoughtfully. 'There's more to that girl than meets the eye. She called him Cedric, did you notice? Not Sir Cedric. I'll bet there was something going on there.'

Midge quietly left the room. Under cover of Lettie's outburst, she had ubobtrusively cleared the fatal table. When they turned to inspect the evidence, it would be gone. This would place her, as 'housekeeper' and person who had done some of the serving, under suspicion as well as the actors.

'It's started, has it?' Cook looked up as Midge returned to the kitchen. 'I saw them carrying Sir Cedric through to the private quarters. They dropped him twice before they got there,' she added with gloomy relish. 'And they couldn't stop and let him walk because a couple of the guests were following them. 'They had to pick him up and carry on. He won't half have some bruises in the morning.'

'Oh dear, poor Cedric.' Midge stacked the cups, saucers and glasses in the dishwasher and switched it on. 'There, that will give them something to worry about.'

Ackroyd sauntered over to her feet and complained bitterly about his continued incarceration in the kitchen.

'Oh, all right,' Midge said, opening the door for him. 'You can go and join the party—but don't get in the way.'

'Well.' Cook rose, responding to some inner clock, crossed to the cooker and began removing trays of fragrant, steaming chicken fillets from the oven. 'I'll just put these in the larder to cool and then I'm going to go to my room and lock myself in. I don't know what kind of people we're getting these days, but there has to be something wrong with them. Whoever heard of spending your holiday pretending a murder has been committed and then chasing around prying into other people's business and lying your own head off?'

'It's become very popular,' Midge defended. 'And thank heaven for it. We'd have had a hard winter without them.'

'I don't know what Mr Eric would have said about all these goings-on.'

'Mr Eric is in Australia, having a wonderful time—and having left all the problems to poor Reggie. He wanted the Manor saved—and we're saving it. We're turning it into a going concern. Admit it now, Cook, isn't it nice to be paid on time?'

Cook was arranging trays on racks in the larder, her reply was indistinct. She emerged, looking flustered but triumphant, and locked the larder door.

'There,' she said, 'that will keep Ackroyd out. Smart as he is, he hasn't learned to unlock doors yet. I'll do a mayonnaise glaze on them first thing in the morning. They'll look a treat for lunch.'

'And they'll *be* a treat. Oh, Cook, you're a treasure. I don't know what we'd do without you.'

'That's as may be.' Cook was obviously pleased. 'I'm not saying it isn't nice to have lots of people to cook for again —just like the house-parties in the old days when Mrs Eric was alive. But I'm still locking myself in tonight. If you ask me, those people out there aren't right in the head!'

'They're just harmless rôle-players, having fun in their own way.'

'Some way!' Cook sniffed and looked round the kitchen. 'Just you keep them out of here. I won't have them poking around and moving things out of their proper places so's I can't find them again.'

'I'll make it clear that the kitchen is out of bounds.' Midge hoped she could enforce that rule. Perhaps it was going to be a mistake, bringing Cook in for a bit part. Would some of the guests follow her back to the kitchen for more questioning after she had drawn herself to their attention? It was awfully hard to predict what they might do. Every tour was different —and this one seemed to be keener than most.

Cook was right, though, there was something especially unsettling about these people, although Midge couldn't quite put her finger on the reason—apart from the Chandler twins. Their open pursuit of Bramwell Barbour was a complication that had not been present on previous tours.

There were muted voices outside the kitchen door. Cook stiffened and watched the door with hostile eyes. Midge moved over to it, prepared to repel boarders.

'Thought we might find you here—' It was only Reggie and Ned, returning from having disposed of Cedric and having momentarily shaken off their pursuers. 'Time to get back and man the bar. All this excitement will be making them thirsty.'

'I suppose so.' Midge followed Reggie back to the bar, Ned trailing behind. As Reggie had expected, there were several eager customers waiting.

'How is he?' Haila Bond demanded as Reggie took his place behind the bar 'How's Sir Cedric?'

'Still indisposed,' Reggie said firmly. 'But he wouldn't want to spoil the party for anyone. Instructions are to carry on as usual.'

'He's dead, isn't he?' Asey Wentworth accused.

'Shhh—' Reggie managed a splendid expression of furtive guilt. 'We mustn't disturb the others. There's nothing anyone can do tonight and we don't want to cast a pall over the festivities.'

'Someone has done too much already.' Dixon Carr fixed Midge with an accusing gaze. 'Why did you clear that table, Midge?'

'It's customary to clear empty tables,' Midge said crisply. 'One can't leave dirty dishes lying about.'

'And where are those cups and glasses you cleared from that table now?'

'In the dishwasher, of course.'

'Of course.' Haila Bond had crowded closer. 'And I suppose you've switched the dishwasher on?'

'Naturally.' Midge was the picture of an innocent house-keeper. 'That's the whole point of having a dishwasher.'

'So that takes care of that,' Asey Wentworth said gloomily.

'And just as well, too.' Bertha Stout pushed her way to the fore. 'We have no way of analysing substances. I say the only way we'll solve this case is through the human element. Who wanted Sir Cedric dead? Who hated him? Who pro-fited? Motivation—that's where your answer lies.' She glanced at Midge absently. 'I'll have a double bourbon. It's going to be a long night.'

The others ordered enthusiastically, as well. Then, clutch-ing their glasses, let the theories begin flying.

'There was something extra in Sir Cedric's coffee. Re-member? When Lettie gave it to him, she said it was just the way he liked it. And they *looked* at each other.'

'When he was dying, he called out for her. Remember? He kept trying to say her name . . . Et . . . Et . . .'

'Aha! But did he mean Lettie—or *Pet*? They both have the *et* sound and he wasn't articulating clearly. Could he have been accusing one of them? And which one?'

'Or maybe he was saying it was something he *et*. That's the way some of them pronounce *ate* over here. Maybe it was the mushroom soup catching up with him. I suspected that soup from the first!'

'How about that ice-cream? Easy enough to slip a bit of cyanide into the Amaretto. The flavour would mask the taste until it was too late—'

'Cyanide is too fast-acting for that. He'd never have made it to the drawing-room if it had been cyanide.'

'Yes, and the gentlemen lingered over port, don't forget. There was a good time-span between both soup and ice-cream before Sir Cedric collapsed. It *must* have been in his coffee or brandy.'

'I still say—' Dixon Carr glared at Midge—'it's too bad that table was cleared. We might have learned something.'

'How?' Bertha asked practically. 'All you could have done was sniff at the cups and glasses. We already know there was something extra in Sir Cedric's coffee. A few sniffs wouldn't have necessarily told you what. None of us are that expert, you know.'

'Here's the only expert sniffer in the place.' Midge bent and picked up Ackroyd, who had just strolled into the bar, having completed his circuit of the drawing-room. 'You could show them a thing or two, couldn't you, Ackroyd?'

'Could he?' Dix quivered with sudden suspicion. 'Are you trying to tell us that cat is an expert witness?'

'Why not? Midge laughed. 'Just look at the way he's shadowing you suspects.'

'Maybe he's heard your nickname is Codfish,' Haila said to Asey Wentworth. 'He's going to try a little nibble.'

'I know what he's after.' Midge set Ackroyd down on the floor and found a saucer for him. 'He's been haunting the bar ever since we started experimenting with exotic cocktails. It didn't take him long to discover there's always a jug of cream back here now. Did it, you little rotter?' She poured cream into the saucer while Ackroyd twined round her ankles.

'Just a minute, Midge.' Dix caught her arm as she began to lower the saucer to the floor. 'Let me see that.' He took the saucer and sniffed at the cream while Midge stared at him incredulously.

'Hmmm . . .' He dipped a forefinger into the cream, sniffed again and gingerly touched it to the tip of his tongue. 'It seems to be all right.' He released her arm. 'You can give it to him now.'

'What on earth—?' Midge looked at Dix blankly.

'Just making sure.' He smiled at her sternly. 'It wouldn't be the first death of an expert witness—and right under the noses of other people. I don't mind losing Sir Cedric, but I'd hate to be party to the murder of Roger Ackroyd.'

CHAPTER 10

'. . . drifts are six feet deep in some parts of the country. Especially hard hit are Wiltshire, Gloucestershire and the West Country. Snow ploughs are being hampered by vehicles left abandoned on the highways . . .'

Midge groaned and opened the other eye.

'And it's still snowing,' Reggie reported from the window. 'That tears it. There's not a hope of getting them in to town this morning and we can scrub the Scavenger Hunt this afternoon. We'll have to find other ways to entertain them.'

'Snowbound—that's all we need!' Midge joined him at the window, struggling into her robe. 'What time did you get to bed last night, anyway?'

'This morning,' he corrected. 'It was already morning when you gave up. I don't know. Sometime around three, I think. Some of them were still sitting around the fire, still deducing. I threw another log on the fire and left them to it. They're certainly going to get their money's worth out of every minute.'

'Perhaps they'll sleep late,' Midge said hopefully.

'Not them, they're too afraid they might miss something. I found a couple of them prowling the kitchen corridor when I went through and had to warn them off. We're going to need a lock for the door to the private wing if we mean to go on with this lark. Too many of them think out-of-bounds just means we're trying to put something over on them.'

'Oh dear.' Midge stared, hypnotized, at the relentlessly falling flakes. 'I hope they don't do anything to upset Cook.'

Cook was furious. She slapped bacon rashers into the grill pan and slammed the pan under the grill. She took her blunt knife and cracked eggs as though they were tourists' heads.

If any of them had seen her, she'd have gone straight to Number One on the list of suspects.

Ackroyd was prudently seated in the farthest corner, out of the way, tail curled tightly around his feet. He watched warily as Cook stormed about the kitchen.

'I won't have it!' Cook raged at Midge as soon as she entered. 'They came in here last night and helped themselves! It's bad enough turning the place into a hotel—but with everybody pretending they're at a private house-party, no one knows where they're at. I won't have them raiding the kitchen for midnight snacks. There's got to be a limit!'

'I quite agree,' Midge soothed. 'But are you sure? I can't imagine anyone would do such a thing.'

'Can't you? Then you just come and see.' Cook unlocked the larder door and threw it open. 'Look at that!'

Midge stepped inside and regarded the trays of chicken fillets. Cook had laid out each tray with geometric precision. It was perfectly clear that three fillets were missing from the top tray. Their outlines remained, limned in jellied juices.

'Now don't try to tell me Ackroyd did it,' Cook said. 'Even though he does look guilty enough.'

Ackroyd paused in the doorway, indeed looking guilty. His ears flattened slightly as Cook spoke his name. He looked from Cook to Midge with narrowed eyes and seemed to sense that this was not a propitious moment to suggest a handout. He backed out of the doorway hastily.

'I'm sorry about this,' Midge said. 'Some of them were running around till all hours this morning. I suppose they got hungry. I'll speak to them and make sure it doesn't happen again.'

'It better not!'

'Anyway, you have enough left to go around, haven't you? There seem to be plenty—'

'Of course I have. That's not the point!'

'No, no, of course not. I was just worried about lunch. We'll have them all here, you know. They won't be able to get into town or go out on a scavenger hunt in this weather.'

'They won't want cold chicken and salad, either. I was thinking I might do a lemon cream sauce and baked potatoes, perhaps with baby carrots and peas.'

'Splendid!' Midge applauded. 'I knew you'd—'

A sharp bell pealed through the kitchen.

'*Her* again!' Cook glanced at the number that had dropped into view. 'It was a sorry day for all of us when she discovered that bell rope.'

'I'll go,' Midge said quickly. 'I suppose she wants breakfast served in her suite.' And anything that kept Amaryllis out of the way of the other guests was to be encouraged. She wasn't exactly the life of the party.

'They're drifting in for breakfast.' Reggie came into the kitchen, squinting at his order pad. 'Four pots of coffee, three of tea. Where are the hot rolls?'

'Ready to come out of the oven.' Cook snapped to attention.

Midge went to answer the bell. She passed Lettie on the servants' staircase.

'I've just shoved the clues under the doors,' Lettie reported. 'I gave the licence to Bertha Stout and the cryptic one to Dixon Carr. They seem to be shaping up as leaders of opposing factions.'

'Good work. Shh—' Midge motioned her to silence. They listened to the muffled footsteps descending the carpeted family staircase on the other side of the wall.

'They're stirring early,' Lettie muttered. 'I nearly got caught—and I couldn't stand another grilling at this hour of the morning.'

'Wait until Bertha finds her clue,' Midge said heartlessly. 'She'll turn you inside out.'

'Don't I know it! Sometimes I—' Lettie broke off, listening. 'Who's that?'

Another set of footsteps—this time descending the inner staircase from somewhere above them, ringing out on the uncarpeted stairs. They waited in silence, looking upwards.

The footsteps rang nearer, a pair of trousered legs came into view.

'Oh, Bram!' Lettie exhaled a long, shuddering breath. 'You frightened us!'

'Did I? I'm sorry. I didn't mean to. I didn't realize there was anyone here. I'm sorry, but—' he looked haunted—'I had to get away.'

'Get away?' Lettie was abruptly alert. 'Away from what?'

'Oh, nothing. Nothing, really. It's just, Mother—' He broke off, glancing upwards guiltily.

'What about your mother?' Lettie's voice was hard.

'She means well.' Bramwell was defensive. 'She just doesn't understand. She—she's invited those women—those *creatures*—to breakfast. With us—in our suite. This morning—now.' His face was blank with the shock of betrayal.

'You mean she's matchmaking,' Lettie said harshly.

'You mustn't blame her.' He seemed to be arguing with himself as much as with Lettie. 'They're very rich, you know. Millions. And millions more to come as elderly relatives die off. They're the last of a long, dying line—'

A family run to seed. The thought sprang into Midge's mind. There was something decadent about the identical women that turned one's thoughts to empty echoing mansions, fluttering cobwebs trailing from peeling gilt splendour, bats whirling through space—Oh yes, bats, indeed.

'Which one does she favour?' Lettie seemed to control herself with great effort.

'Oh, I don't think she cares. They both have money. Either one would do.' Bramwell shuddered. 'It doesn't matter—to her.'

'That's monstrous!' Midge exclaimed.

'Oh, you mustn't blame her too much. You don't understand—it was so hard after my father died and before I began earning. We really struggled. Even now, with things going so well, she's always afraid. She wants to see me secure against the ups and downs, the books that might not do so well, the statements when the royalties are down. She only wants security for me—for us.'

'For which—' Lettie was quivering with rage—'she'd sell you, body and soul, to those harpies!'

'Please—' Bramwell winced. 'I told you you wouldn't understand. She means so well—'

'Smuggle him into the kitchen,' Midge instructed Lettie, 'and give him breakfast. Then he can join Cedric in the private wing. He can help Cedric paste up the poison pen letters for tonight. We'll cover for him and say he's working on his new book and can't be disturbed.'

'Oh, thank you,' Bramwell said gratefully.

'Just come along.' Lettie took his hand. 'And tiptoe. We don't want the guests to discover this passage until we're ready for them.'

Midge continued on her way upstairs to take Amaryllis's orders for breakfast. She was going to enjoy this.

'Orange juice for four,' Amaryllis ordered. 'Scrambled eggs and back. Toast and marmalade. Coffee.'

'Just think,' Lauren Chandler said to her twin. 'We've spent the night under the same roof with Bramwell Barbour. And—'

'And now we're going to have breakfast with him,' Brigid finished.

'And it won't be long until—' They looked at each other. Something predatory stirred behind their vacant glittering eyes. They both giggled.

'Now, girls,' Amaryllis said indulgently. 'Not too noisy, you'll wake him up. We want this to be a surprise, don't we?'

'Oh yes.' They stifled their giggles, glancing anxiously towards the closed bedroom door. 'But where is he? Does he always sleep this late?'

'Don't worry,' Amaryllis said. 'There's plenty of time. All the time in the world.'

'There sure is.' Brigid glanced towards the window and the falling snow. 'Did you hear the weather forecast? We may all be snowed in here together for days—weeks, even.'

Midge abruptly stopped enjoying the situation. She hadn't really considered that. If this snow continued, there was little likelihood that the tour would be able to depart on schedule tomorrow afternoon. They could be stuck here for several more days.

The snow ploughs would clear the arterial routes first, then the main highways. It could be a couple of days before they reached the lesser roads—if they bothered about them at all.

'I'll see to your breakfast,' Midge told Amaryllis—and fled.

This time she used the main staircase, nodding absently in response to the greetings of guests descending to the dining-room for breakfast. She glanced into the dining-room as she passed and saw Reggie industriously serving breakfast. The guests had gravitated to the same tables they had been assigned last night, so the actors had obligingly switched tables in order that a different group might question them—if anyone felt up to it so early in the morning.

In the kitchen, Cedric and Bramwell sat at a table in the corner, sharing their eggs and bacon with Ackroyd, who was perched on the third chair at their table, graciously accepting all offerings as no more than his rightful due.

'You'll be dying of thirst all day, if you eat any more bacon.' Midge pulled back the chair and tipped Ackroyd out of it. She took his place and accepted the coffee Cedric automatically poured for her.

'What did she want?' Cook asked ominously.

'Breakfast, as we thought. For four. Coffee, scrambled eggs, bacon, orange juice and toast.'

'Make that for three,' Bramwell said. 'I'm not going to be there.'

'We're not supposed to know that,' Midge pointed out. 'We'll have to play it straight and bring up breakfast for four.' Let Amaryllis find out for herself that the bird had flown. In fact . . . 'Reggie can do it.'

'Reggie can do what?' He came through from the dining-room, looking harassed.

'I'm afraid Mother wants breakfast in her rooms,' Bramwell apologized. 'And you haven't seen me.'

'Wheels within wheels—as usual.' Reggie consulted the scribblings on his order pad, trying to sort them out. 'I think that says poached eggs—' He shrugged at Cook. 'I don't know why I'm worrying. They've found their clues and they're so excited they won't know if they're eating eggs or aubergines. They just want to get hold of Lettie and begin firing questions at her. Where is she?'

'She's probably preparing for her big entrance,' Midge said.

'Thank God they can't get at me.' Cedric shuddered. 'Lettie can remember all those ins-and-outs. Comes of having a trained mind. They'd trip me up every time.'

'That's why we murdered you first,' Reggie said cheerfully. 'Eliminate the weakest link before it breaks—first rule of the game. You can't say we haven't learned fast.'

'Hermione actually enjoys all this,' Cedric grumbled. 'You can't tell me she doesn't. She's having the time of her life in there right now, starting up hares and shooting down red herrings. I never knew she had it in her.'

'She's doing a wonderful job,' Midge said warmly. 'I don't know how we'd have managed without her.'

'Don't know how you're going to manage anyway, with this weather.' Cedric looked over his shoulder. The snow was still falling. 'Hasn't half mucked up the schedule, what?'

'We'll just have to bring events forward.' Midge had been considering the problem. 'Since they can't have a scavenger hunt, we'll just have to murder Hermione after lunch instead of after dinner. Then Lettie can be killed—after she finishes serving dinner.'

'Make it after she finishes clearing away the dishes,' Reggie suggested. 'We're going to be short-handed enough. The help from the village won't be able to struggle through in this storm. In fact, it might be better if we kept Lettie alive. How about another victim? Do you think Miss Holloway might oblige?'

'She'd love it, I'm sure, but that would send the plot-line up the creek. How would we explain her murder?'

'Bramwell ought to be able to think of something,' Reggie said. 'If we can't explain an extra body with two of the best brains in the business on the premises, when can we? You'll help, won't you, Bram?'

'Of course.' Bram frowned thoughtfully. 'No problem at all. Everyone already suspects Miss Holloway is part of the show. She can simply drop a few hints that she knows too much and—there you are. The perfect reason for murdering her—for murdering anybody. Absolutely classic.'

'Wonderful!' Midge applauded. 'I'll have a word with Grace and we'll tip off the actors. That should take up the slack in the schedule.'

'What about the anonymous letters, then?' Cedric grumbled. 'Will that change the wording of them? I've collected just enough newsprint to do them the way we've planned. It's going to be tricky if we need to add extra words.'

'Oh dear.' Midge hadn't thought of that. 'Why don't you and Bramwell start pasting and let him decide? We might be able to get away with the original wording.'

A bell pealed sharply and demandingly, setting the dropped number card clattering in its little box. Bramwell and Cedric jumped, but the others knew only too well what it was.

'Taking too long to suit her,' Cook said bitterly, then abruptly remembered that Bramwell was present. She gave the number a dark look and moved off to fill the plates set out on the tray.

'I'll take it up, shall I?' Lettie appeared from the private wing, her make-up refreshed, looking ready for battle.

'Reggie will do that,' Midge said quickly. 'You and I will take care of the dining-room.'

CHAPTER 11

'Lettie!' All eyes turned to stare at her. 'Here's Lettie now. What does she have to say about it?'

'Good morning.' Smiling placidly, Lettie advanced to the nearest table, the one filled with the undemanding guests who were just along for the ride. It was a nice try, but she didn't get away with it.

'Lettie!' Bertha Stout called her over to her table. 'Lettie—' She waved a piece of paper at her—'do you know anything about this? It was pushed under my door this morning.'

'What—?' Lettie snatched for the piece of paper, but Bertha pulled it back out of her reach. 'Where did you get that?'

'I just told you. It was pushed under my door this morning. You recognize it, don't you?'

'No!' Lettie said frantically; she did it very well. 'I never saw it before in my life. It's a forgery!'

'If you never saw it before and you don't know what it is, how can you say it's a forgery?' Asey Wentworth pounced. 'Got you there!'

'What is it?' someone called from an adjoining table. 'What have you found?'

'Evidence,' Bertha said triumphantly. 'It's an application for a marriage licence—made out to Sir Cedric Strangeways and Letitia Heyer, Spinster of this Parish.'

'And it's two months old,' Asey pointed out. 'How about it, Lettie? Did you get the old boy to go through with it? Is there a marriage certificate hidden away somewhere? Are you really Lady Strangeways?'

'That's no concern of yours!' Lettie flared.

'Lettie!' Lady Hermione rose from her table and stalked

over to confront her. 'Is this true? What have you to say for yourself, girl?'

'Don't you *girl* me, your high-and-mighty Ladyship. I'm as good as you are!' Lettie hurled her tray down on the table and rushed from the room.

'Come back here! Don't you run away when I'm speaking to you!' Lady Hermione chased after her.

'I don't understand—' Alice Dain said into the momentary silence that followed. 'Did she marry him, or didn't she? Is she Lady Strangeways? Is that what she meant when she said she was as good as Lady Hermione?'

'If she married him, then this place ought to belong to her now. So why is she still wearing her maid's uniform and waiting on us?'

'To throw us off the track. If she inherits, that gives her a motive for doing away with him.'

'But if she hadn't married him yet, it would give Lady Hermione a motive for getting rid of her brother before he was able to marry Lettie. Lady Hermione would hate having a maid for her sister-in-law—and *she'd* inherit if Sir Cedric was still a bachelor when he died.'

'Unless he left a Will saying otherwise. Has anyone heard anything about a Will?'

Theories were flying thick and fast. Only the table occupied by Dixon Carr and his cohorts refrained from adding to the din. When the first outburst had died down, if only to allow the guests to eat their breakfast while it was still hot—Dix cleared his throat.

'I wouldn't want to detract from your triumph—' He leaned across the space between their tables and addressed Bertha. 'But I found a little something slipped beneath my own door this morning.'

'The marriage certificate?' Bertha was instantly jealous of her personal clue.

'No, no. Not so dramatic as yours, I admit.' He paused. 'But food for thought.' He unfolded a small slip of paper and smiled at it. 'Definitely food for thought.'

'Tell them,' Haila Bond prodded eagerly. 'Read it out to them.'

'It just says: *Et tu, Brute?* Now, doesn't that make you think?'

'Think what?' Bertha sniffed. 'It's too cryptic to be of any use.'

'Is it?' Dix nodded as though his private estimate of her intelligence had been confirmed. 'Think of Sir Cedric's last words: *Et . . . et.* I believe that this is what he was trying to say: *Et tu, Brute?*'

There was an impressed silence.

'But who's *Brute?*' Alice Dain wailed.

'Would you like to answer that, young man?' Dix turned to Edwin Lupin.

'You're way ahead of me, sir,' Ned confessed with an easy grin. 'I'll tell you one thing, it wasn't me. I'd never seen the old boy before yesterday. I certainly don't qualify as Brutus to his who-ever-it-was.'

'Cæsar,' Dix said. 'Julius Cæsar—one of the greatest Generals in the history of mankind. And Sir Cedric was a military historian. At his moment, his thoughts turned to the parallel—the betrayal of Caesar by the friend he trusted.'

'What friend?' Bertha demanded. 'We're all strangers to him. He was sitting at the bridge table with his sister and Petronella—he wouldn't call either of them Brutus. And Edwin had never met him before.'

'Aha!' Dix nodded maddeningly. 'I hope to have more information about that before the day is over.'

'You mean you hope something else will be pushed under your door,' Bertha said witheringly.

Before Dix could reply, a bloodcurdling scream resounded through the hallway outside, accompanied by sounds of pounding feet, then another scream.

This was unscheduled. Midge took a firmer grip on her tray and waited; her nerves had toughened immeasurably in recent weeks.

'He's gone! Gone!' One of the Chandler twins appeared in the doorway, hysterical.

'He isn't in his room! He isn't anywhere!' Her twin pushed her aside and howled out her news. 'Bramwell Barbour has disappeared!'

Bertha and Dix threw down their napkins and were neck-and-neck racing for the doorway.

'Are you sure?' Bertha demanded.

'Has his bed been slept in?' Dix wanted to know.

'Yes,' one of the twins wailed. 'But I'm sure he wasn't in it for long. He—he's gone!'

'Now take it easy.' Dix looked over her shoulder and addressed his next question to Amaryllis, who has just appeared. 'Is this true?'

'It's true,' she said grimly. 'Bramwell has disappeared. He must have gone during the night. I didn't see him or hear him this morning. When I knocked on his door and went in—he wasn't there.'

'He can't have gone far,' Bertha said. 'Not in this storm.'

'I didn't like to say anything—' Haila Bond was clearly delighted to be able to bear witness—'but I heard footsteps in the middle of the night. Footsteps where they couldn't have been—inside the walls. I was going to ask if the place was haunted.'

'It isn't,' Midge said firmly. Someone must have been careless using the servants' passage.

'Then maybe it was Bramwell Barbour I heard. Maybe he walks in his sleep.'

'He's never done that before,' Amaryllis said coldly.

'There's a first time for everything.' Bertha frowned. 'But where could he have gone? Did you check outside?'

'We looked out of all the windows,' Brigid choked. 'We couldn't see anything.'

'*You* couldn't,' Lauren said. 'I saw a trail of hollows in the snow, like footprints filled in by fresh snow. I think we ought to follow them. He may be lying out there—buried in the drifts.'

'Excuse me,' Stanley Marric interrupted, a wicked gleam in his eyes. 'But has anyone noticed that Evelina T. Carterslee isn't here, either? Maybe they've run off together.'

'Don't be absurd,' Amaryllis snapped. 'Why, she's old enough to be—'

His mother? Unspoken, the thought hung heavy in the air that Bramwell was perhaps more comfortable in the company of older women.

'That's silly!' Lauren was furious. 'Why, Bramwell's engaged to us—or as good as.'

'Us?' Dixon Carr blinked. 'Surely you mean one or the other of you.'

'Oh, sure. Either one.' The twins exchanged glances and tittered. 'It doesn't matter. We share everything.'

'I should think that the gentleman concerned might have something to say about that.' Dix regarded them with severe disapproval.

'Him? He can't tell us apart, anyway.' They tittered again. 'No one can. He'll never know the difference.'

'And you, madam—' Dix turned his stern gaze on Amaryllis. 'Do you approve these plans for a *ménage à trois*? With your own son as an unknowing victim?'

'Oh, they're just being silly little girls,' Amaryllis said indulgently. 'They don't really mean it. They're only trying to shock you.'

'They've succeeded,' Dix said.

The Chandler twins meant it. Amaryllis must be the only person within earshot who didn't believe them. Of course, she wouldn't, would she? She could not admit to herself that she was willing to sell her son into that sort of slavery. Midge felt new sympathy for Bramwell. He had more problems than she had thought—and she'd been aware that he had plenty.

'Oh! Why are we standing here?' Brigid exploded. 'We've got to find him! Let's make up two search parties—one for outdoors and one for inside the house. We've got to find him!'

'One last question,' Dix said. 'How did you—I mean, you two—happen to discover he was missing?'

'We were going to have breakfast with him. Amaryllis invited us. We waited and waited for him to wake up. When he didn't, we opened his door—and he was gone!'

'Umm-hmm . . .' Glances were exchanged, several people began to drift back to their abandoned breakfasts. Suddenly, there wasn't quite so much mystery about Bramwell Barbour's disappearance. He had a motive none of them could quarrel with—they would have leaped out of a window themselves, if necessary, to escape breakfast with the Chandler twins.

'We're wasting time!' Lauren said. 'He could be lying hurt somewhere—dying!'

Some of the others were becoming uneasy again. There was just the possibility . . .

'Those footsteps I heard—' Haila Bond's eyes snapped avidly. 'They were going upstairs. To the attic.'

'That's a clue, if I ever heard one.' Dix grasped it eagerly. No one was anxious to go out and blunder about in the storm just to quiet the twins' hysterical fears. 'Suppose we search the house first? If we don't find him in here, then we can think about looking outside.'

'Great idea.' Stanley Marric was enthusiastic. He glanced towards the windows and shivered involuntarily. 'We're bound to find him inside somewhere.'

Midge was sure of it. If necessary, she would kick him out of his sanctuary herself.

'But if he *is* outside—' The Chandler twins remained unconvinced. 'If he is, he could be frozen to death while we're searching in here in the warmth.' Lauren didn't realize it, but she had just blown her argument. Reminded afresh of the blizzard outside and the comfort within, the searchers were unanimous in their determination to begin inside—and stay inside.

'We'll start with the attic,' Haila said. 'That was where those footsteps were heading.'

'Not only that,' Dix backed her, 'but it's the correct way to search a house. From the top down.'

'I still think we ought to start outside,' Lauren protested. 'Just because Haila has been hearing ghosts is no reason—'

'There are no ghosts in Chortlesby Manor,' Midge said.

'There are always ghosts in a place like this.' Brigid was equally firm. 'You're just trying to keep it from us because you think we'd be scared.'

Midge opened her mouth, then closed it again. Let them believe what they liked. The main thing was that the search could replace the scavenger hunt and keep them occupied until the next murder.

Roberta Rinehart was in the kitchen, looking inordinately happy, when Midge returned. The night's sleep seemed to have accomplished a minor miracle.

'I couldn't face the hordes at this hour,' she greeted Midge cheerfully. 'I'm hiding out here until I have time to wake up. Cook's taking care of me wonderfully. I told her I only wanted toast and coffee, but she's insisting I have the full English breakfast.'

'Quite right,' Midge said absently. 'You'll need to be well fortified to put up with them this morning. They're searching the house right now.'

'Whatever for?'

'Bramwell Barbour has disappeared.'

'That was sporting of him.' Roberta looked thoughtful. 'Or should I say cowardly?'

'Cowardly, by all means. He's behind the scenes with Cedric, escaping the Chandler twins.'

'I see.' Roberta sighed. 'I did feel a bit guilty about that, I must admit. But what could I do? They insisted on joining the tour—and heaven knows they have enough money. I couldn't refuse to take them just because it would upset Bram. Let his mother protect him from them.'

'His mother appears to be on their side.'

'In that case, he's just going to have to grow up and fight

his own battles.' Roberta shrugged off Bramwell's troubles, obviously in too good a mood to let anything disturb her. She stretched luxuriously, raising her arms full-length above her head, and giggled.

'What are you so pleased about?' Midge was instantly suspicious. The difference between Roberta last night and Roberta this morning was so dramatic that it could hardly be accounted for by just a good night's sleep.

'Why shouldn't I be? I've had a lovely sleep, a delicious breakfast—and it's a beautiful day!'

'You call this blizzard beautiful? Don't you realize you're all going to be stranded here for heaven knows how long?'

'Yes,' Roberta gurgled joyously. 'Isn't it wonderful?'

'Wonderf—? Roberta, is there something you'd like to tell me?'

'I'll tell you—' Roberta's eyes were dancing—'but, for heaven's sake, don't tell anyone else. I've been worried sick for the past couple of days. The charter company let us down. They suddenly notified me that they couldn't supply a plane to fly us home tomorrow night. If we had to re-book the tour on to commercial flights, it would eat up most of our profits and we'd probably have had to split up the tour and send them on different planes. It would have upset everyone and spoiled the whole tour for them. Now, we're saved! We can't be blamed for a blizzard. Another couple of days and the charter company will have a plane available and the tour will never know.' She suddenly looked concerned.

'It *is* all right, isn't it? You have enough food—?'

'Plenty,' Midge said. 'The freezer is well-stocked. Depending on how long we're snowed up, the food may get a bit monotonous, but there'll be enough of it.'

'Good.' Roberta sighed with relief. 'Don't worry, we'll make it up to you on the price. You won't lose by it.'

'I'm not worried,' Midge said truthfully. A couple of extra days of the cash bar would bring a hefty profit. Happily, this was a fairly heavy-drinking crowd. Or perhaps the

Thirties theme, with its reminder of Prohibition, was encouraging them to drink more.

'Good. Then we have nothing to worry about.'

Loud hysterical screams suddenly resounded from somewhere above them.

'Nothing—' Midge said grimly—'except the possibility that one of us may do actual murder before this crowd leaves. Come on, let's go and see what they're taking on about now.'

CHAPTER 12

'We saw it! We saw it!' Brigid squealed. 'We saw your ghost!'

'*You* saw it—you think,' Lauren said. 'I didn't see anything.'

'It was there—right ahead of us. And then it wasn't!'

'It wasn't there at all. You were seeing things. You know you're too high-strung—you always were.'

'I wasn't. I'm not. It was there—a tall pale brown man in a navy blue shroud.'

'You're sure it wasn't a grey flannel shroud?' Even Dix had a hard time keeping a straight face.

'Or crimson?' Haila asked meaningly.

'You're all laughing at me,' Brigid pouted. 'I saw it, I tell you. I could draw you a picture of it, except it disappeared so fast. Into thin air.'

'Best place for it,' Bertha Stout said sensibly. 'Now stop worrying about it and let's get on with the search. We're looking for Bramwell Barbour—not ghosts.'

'Besides, it's daylight,' Haila said. 'Spirit manifestations usually occur between dusk and dawn. It was well after the witching hour when I heard those footsteps.'

'That just shows how much *you* know.' Brigid was still sulking. 'It didn't make any sound at all. So there.'

'Whatever it was, it isn't here now,' Stanley Marric said impatiently. 'Let's get on with the search. We have two more floors to cover—and I suppose there's a cellar?'

'It's mostly a wine cellar,' Midge said. 'I'd rather you didn't go in there. We don't want the wines disturbed.'

'There's too much out-of-bounds around here,' Haila complained. 'I don't see how we can do a proper job when half the Manor is closed to us.'

'Stan's right, we're wasting time,' Asey Wentworth said. 'We've got to find our favourite author. Why, poor Mrs Barbour must be worried sick.'

'I am,' Amaryllis agreed through clenched teeth. She did not seem terribly worried. The expression on her face boded ill for Bramwell when he was found.

'Anyway,' Dix said, 'we've done this floor. Let's go on to the floor below—and keep a sharp eye out. That's the floor he disappeared from.'

The sound of typing rose to meet them as they descended the stairs. They exchanged glances and quickened their steps.

'He's back!' the twins cried and raced each other down the stairs. 'Bram! Bram!' They hammered on the door of the Barbour suite. 'Where have you been?'

'I'm afraid—' Midge cut short their rapture—'that's Mrs Carterslee you hear typing. She works on her new book every day until lunch-time.'

'Does she?' Sheer malice glinted in Amaryllis's eyes. 'Of course,' she said thoughtfully, 'I suppose Bramwell might be in there with her.'

The twins promptly switched their attention to Evelina's door. The typing faltered to a halt.

'What *is* it?' Evelina opened the door, looking both abstracted and distracted. 'Is the place on fire?'

'Worse!' Brigid said dramatically. 'Bramwell is missing!'

'Oh, really?' The news seemed to strike Evelina as something less than earth-shaking. 'What do you expect me to do about it?'

'We want to search your rooms—' Boldly Lauren pushed against the door and stepped forward. 'We're looking *every-where* for him.'

'Well, you won't find him here.' Evelina tried to stem the relentless advance.

'He might have slipped in without your noticing.' Brigid stepped sideways and through the gap as her twin pushed at the door. Automatically, the others followed, until they were all inside the sitting-room and Evelina had retreated to guard her desk and manuscript.

'Do what you want to do,' she said in exasperation. 'And then get out. I'm trying to work.'

'So wise of you,' Amaryllis murmured. 'The critics all said your last one could have used a lot more work.'

'Were those the same critics who recommended a diet of saltpetre and tranquillizers for Adam MacAdam and Suzie Chong? I must say I agreed. Bram is going to go straight from the mystery lists to the porn lists—with never a stop at Mainstream—if he isn't more careful.'

'Speaking as a mere reader and fan—' Dix interrupted the exchange. 'I have been thrilled to find both of my favourite authors under the same roof—and to discover that they have been in such close proximity for some weeks. It makes me wonder if I dare hope that they might have been collaborating? I can't tell you the thrill it would be for us fans to think that we could look forward to having Luigi von Murphy, Adam MacAdam and Suzie Chong appearing in the same book—working on the same case.'

'I hardly think our styles—' Evelina began.

'That's not a bad idea.' Amaryllis cut her off. 'It could be quite provocative—and lucrative. Luigi von Murphy meets Suzie Chong . . .' A far-away expression crept over her face as she contemplated the possibilities. 'That poor, frustrated quasi-monk, blossoming like a jungle flower when exposed to the understanding, the warmth, the generosity of Suzie Chong. It has distinct possibilities.'

'I don't think—' Evelina said.

'Yes, yes, I can see it now.' Amaryllis closed her eyes, her face rapt. 'Luigi von Murphy has never met a woman like Suzie before. She will inspire him—release him. He will create a liqueur especially for her—and then a perfume. And he will know that it is his last perfume. No other woman will ever be able to inspire him so again. For Luigi, she will always be *the* woman!'

Her eyes still closed, Amaryllis was unable to observe that Evelina had turned an interesting shade of puce.

'And, of course,' Dix prompted, 'Adam MacAdam would understand?' Was there a wicked gleam in his eye?

'Adam MacAdam *always* understands,' Amaryllis said.

'I have an even better idea,' Evelina said dangerously. 'As *I* visualize it, that pagan trollop and her married-in-name-only paramour have never met anyone like Luigi von Murphy before. After such a close encounter with the goodness, the kindliness, the *saintliness* of Luigi, they see the error of their ways and repent. They forswear their wicked lives and retire, Adam MacAdam to a monastery, and Suzie Chong to a nunnery. And how about a touch of Abelard and Heloise—Bram has plagiarized from practically everyone else in the history of erotica? In true repentance—not to mention striking another blow for militant feminism—and also, since neither of them appears to have a relative to their names, Suzie castrates Adam herself. After all, she's done everything else with and to a man!'

'How dare you?' Amaryllis snarled.

'I really do think—' Midge tried to intervene—'that it's time for—'

'He isn't here,' Brigid reported, re-entering from Evelina's bedroom.

'He's not here, either.' Lauren emerged from the spare bedroom, a cheated expression on her face. 'We'll just have to keep on searching.'

'It's nearly lunch-time,' Midge announced firmly. 'Why don't you go to your own rooms and freshen up? I'm sure

Bramwell will be back soon. He might even be in the dining-room when you go in for lunch.'

'He'd better be.' Stan caught Midge's arm and spoke softly. 'I think I ought to tell you that I'm a lawyer in real life and if you let those crazy broads stampede us out into that storm and somebody catches pneumonia, I will personally handle the lawsuit when they sue you. Fun is fun, but you can't carry on the game to the detriment of the health of the players. If you've got Bramwell Barbour hidden away in the private quarters, I suggest you whistle him up before the game gets out of hand.'

'Oh, really,' Midge said faintly. 'I'm sure Bramwell will appear for lunch.'

'He'd better,' Stanley Marric said grimly and moved away.

'Take it easy.' Now Dix grasped her arm. 'He's only trying to frighten you.'

'He's succeeded,' Midge said. 'We couldn't cope with a lawsuit. It would wipe us out. We'd be—' She broke off. There was no need to admit how close to the wind they were sailing.

'Take it easy,' Dix said again. His face was stern. 'There's entirely too much litigation in the States, most of it unnecessary. I don't think he'd have a leg to stand on, anyway. You aren't forcing your guests out into the storm. If they're crazy enough to let a pair of feeble-minded neurotics order them about, that's their problem. They're all adults, they can always say no.'

'They seem to think it's part of the game,' Midge said. 'But it isn't—honestly. Bram was just escaping from those ghastly females for a while. Only they've set up this hue and cry and are trying to chase him down.'

'Blood sports,' Dix muttered, 'I was always against them.' He released her arm and gave her an encouraging pat on the shoulder. 'Don't you worry. It's not going to happen.'

'I'll guarantee that,' Midge said. 'Bramwell is going to make an appearance at lunch—whether he likes it or not.'

'That's the spirit.' Another encouraging pat.

'I don't care!' On the far side of the room, fresh trouble had erupted. 'You can do what you want—but I'm not giving up. I'm not eating, either!' Brigid stormed towards the door. 'I'm not deserting Bramwell in his hour of need!'

'Neither am I!' Lauren was right behind her. 'But I don't see why we can't eat first. It won't do Bram any good if we collapse.'

Some of the others had already left, Midge noticed. Those who remained were standing around irresolutely while the combatants glared at each other.

'Now that you've searched my rooms—' Evelina seemed close to real-life murder as she spoke icily—'perhaps you'd be good enough to leave me in peace to get on with my work. I was hoping to finish a chapter before lunch.'

'We do apologize,' Dix said earnestly. 'I can assure you, we were not the moving spirits in this intrusion.'

Evelina nodded coldly. She was not interested in who had started the invasion, she was only interested in ending it.

'Lunch will be served in half an hour,' Midge announced firmly.

It worked. There was a concerted rush for the door. Evelina slammed it only slightly behind them.

'It's all right,' Lettie greeted Midge as she entered the kitchen. 'We've done all the rooms, but Grace is fairly knackered now. How about letting her get murdered before Hermione? She could use the rest.'

'All right,' Midge said, 'but make it after tea, rather than lunch. I think everyone could do with a quiet interval. They've been racing around searching for Bramwell.'

'Not all of them,' Lettie said. 'The sensible ones have been stretched out in front of the fire, catching up with their Thirties paperbacks. Some of them have even been playing bridge. And Bram's had a lovely peaceful morning helping Cedric.'

'Yes, but I'm afraid his peace is over. If he doesn't put

in an appearance at lunch, they're planning to search for him outside—'

A gust of wind hurled snow against the window-panes with a slapping sound. It was worse than ever out there.'

'And we can't have that,' Midge finished. 'They don't know their way around. If any of them got lost in this blizzard . . .' She shuddered.

'I take your point,' Lettie said, 'but it does seem hard lines on poor Bram, to throw him to those—those wolverines.'

'Nevertheless,' Midge said firmly, 'if it comes to a choice between him and us, it's going to be him. I've already been warned that we'll be sued if anyone catches pneumonia.'

'You're right—it's going to be him.' Reggie had come up behind them silently. 'You're a nice girl, Lettie, and your kind heart does you credit, but if you want to save Bramwell from a fate worse than death, you're going to have to make an honest man of him and marry him yourself. Why don't we announce the engagement at lunch?'

'Don't even joke about it!' Midge was aghast. 'Those Chandler harpies would tear her limb from limb. I don't think they're normal.'

'Not to mention his mother,' Lettie said. 'We could use another diversion—but not that much of a one.'

The sharp peal of the bell startled them all, then Reggie swore briefly.

'We'll disconnect it while she's at lunch,' Midge said quickly. 'This is too much. We can't cope with her demands as well as those of a houseful of guests—'

'Impossible,' Reggie said flatly.

'I'll explain to her myself—' Midge broke off, realizing that that was not what Reggie had meant. She followed his gaze to the number swinging in its little box.

'Impossible,' he said again. 'That room's unoccupied.'

'Oh dear. It must be those Chandler twins. They'll be barging into the private quarters next.'

'Let me go up there.' Lettie started for the door. 'I'll give them the scare of their useless lives!'

'Ignore it,' Midge said. 'We haven't time now. We've got to start serving lunch.'

'You still have a few minutes,' Reggie said. 'Most of them are still in the bar. I just came out for more ice.' He opened the fridge and began filling the ice bucket.

'Suppose you break it to Bram,' Midge suggested to Lettie, 'that Workers' Playtime is over. He's on duty in the dining-room—as of now.'

Later, in the dining-room, the Chandler twins blissfully fussed over Bramwell. 'But where were you hiding?' Brigid pouted accusingly. 'We looked everywhere.'

'I was working,' Bramwell said curtly.

His mother regarded him with a speculative eye, which he refused to meet. He was also stubbornly deaf to the jokes being made at his expense.

Reggie poured wine lavishly into the waiting glasses, as though it were liquid sunshine to make up for the storm outside. Midge and Lettie raced between kitchen and dining-room, trays piled high with serving dishes.

'I say—' A plaintive voice spoke from the doorway. A tall, thin, bronzed man stood there. 'Doesn't anyone answer bells around here any more?'

All conversation stopped, all eyes turned towards him.

'It's him!' Brigid screamed. 'It's the ghost! I'm going to faint!'

'Don't be stupid,' her twin said. 'You can't see through him. He's as alive as you or me. I think.'

'What—?' The man fell back a step, looking around wildly.

'I know who he is.' Bertha Stout rose to her feet. 'Look at that tan!' She pointed. 'He's the tea planter from Ceylon. He's Petronella's father!'

'Daddy!' Petronella took up the cue. She pushed back her chair and rushed to throw her arms about the stranger. 'Oh, Daddy, darling! You're here!'

The man fell back under her onslaught. Midge and Reggie

closed in on each side of him, took his arms, and rushed
him into the kitchen.

CHAPTER 13

'For God's sake, Dad,' Reggie said. 'What the hell are you
doing here?'

'Don't overwhelm me with affection,' Eric said bitterly.
'I might get above myself.'

'Well, of course, we're glad to see you,' Midge said. 'We
just never expected it. How did you get in? When did you
arrive? Why didn't you let us know?'

'I wanted to surprise you,' Eric said. 'I flew into Heathrow
and hired a car. Then I found I was driving straight into a
storm. It got worse and worse. Finally, I was obliged to
abandon the car and continue on foot—' He flapped a hand
towards the window framing the blizzard. 'It's still out there
somewhere.'

'Impeding the snow ploughs,' Midge murmured.

'Fortunately, I was quite near by then, but it was very
late. The Manor was dark when I arrived. I let myself in
with my own key, had a snack—'

'The three missing chicken fillets—' It was all becoming
clear. 'You ate them!'

'Not all of them,' Eric said defensively. 'I shared one with
a friendly cat. He's new since my time, but seems very
pleasant. In fact, that's how I knew where to find them. He
led me over to the larder and looked so hopeful I knew there
must be something good inside.'

'Trust Ackroyd!' Midge said. 'No wonder he looked so
guilty. He *was* to blame for them going missing.'

'Then I went up to bed,' Eric continued. 'I didn't want
to disturb you in the family wing, so I checked the register
for an empty room and went up the service staircase to it.'

'Producing the ghostly footsteps where they shouldn't be.'

Reggie grinned across at Midge. 'No wonder we've been dogged by the supernatural today. I suppose—'he addressed his father—'you utilized the service passage to disappear into when the hunting party almost caught up with you in the upper corridor?'

'Now that you've brought it up,' Eric said, 'I've been meaning to ask you: what's going on here? When I left it to you, this was a perfectly respectable family hotel. Why have you hired it out as a lunatic asylum? Who are all these mad screaming females? And who was that demented girl who hurled herself at my head and called me Daddy?'

'About that—' Reggie said. 'Now that they've spotted you, I'm afraid you're going to have to resign yourself to the fact that she *is* your daughter, the Honourable Petronella Van Dine. Bertha is right—it's the only explanation. Especially with that tan.'

'What's wrong with my tan? Why should I claim a complete stranger as a daughter? Who are all these—?'

'Hard cheese, old boy.' Cedric had strolled into the kitchen and was grinning evilly at his brother-in-law. 'You've walked right into the middle of it and you'll have to take the consequences. You'll be lucky if you're not done away with before the weekend is over. I was.'

'What are you talking about?'

'Don't pay any attention to Cedric,' Reggie said. 'He's dead.'

'What?'

'Perfectly true, old boy. I turned up my toes after the mushroom soup last night. Unless there was something in the coffee.'

'You're raving mad,' Eric said flatly. 'The lot of you.'

'It's really quite simple,' Midge said. 'Let me explain. We've got a murder on this weekend. Cedric doesn't count —he's dead now—but he was Hermione's brother—'

'He's her husband.' Eric fought weakly for his sanity. '*I'm* her brother.'

'No, you're just an old friend. I'm the housekeeper here

and Reggie is butler-barman-major domo. The Hon. Petronella is your daughter and Lady Hermione is sponsoring her for the London Season. She's doing it because you're such an old friend of hers and you can't do it because you're a widowed tea planter in Ceylon—'

Midge raced through the explanation, aware of modified uproar in the dining-room. She got to her feet. It was time to serve dessert and hope that would keep them occupied for a while.

'There now—' She smiled encouragingly at her father-in-law. 'Got it?'

'I don't want it,' Eric bleated.

'Don't worry,' Cedric said. 'I'll go over his lines with him. He'll have it by tea-time.'

'It won't matter if he's a bit vague—' Midge tried to reassure herself as much as the others. If Cedric was going to work with Eric, it would be the blind leading the blind. 'He won't have to be up on everything that's been happening. He's been out in Ceylon all these years.'

'You keep babbling about Ceylon,' Eric complained. 'What's happened to Sri Lanka?'

'Sri Lanka hasn't happened yet,' Midge threw back over her shoulder. 'This is 1935.'

As she went through the door, she saw Eric slump forward to rest his head on his forearms, moaning, 'The inmates have taken over the asylum.'

'Good to see old Eric again.' Wearing thin rubber kitchen gloves, Colonel Heather had smeared the blade of the carving knife with copious blood. Now he squinted at it thoughtfully. 'He's looking very well.'

'If a bit confused.' Midge dipped into the bucket of blood and arranged a neat coagulation between Grace Holloway's shoulder-blades.

'Well, of course, it's confusing.' Grace wriggled as the stuff seeped through to her skin. 'It must be like walking in in the middle of a film—in the days when they had continuous performances. Cedric will straighten him out.'

'Hah!' The Colonel snorted. 'I'd hate to bet Cedric's got it straight himself yet.'

'Anyway,' Grace said complacently, 'I dropped dark and sinister hints all through lunch. I think I've got them worried about me. One of them warned me that it wasn't safe to let people think I might know too much. I said I'd tell everything I know at dinner tonight—' She giggled. 'Then four of them tried to follow me to protect me—but I gave them the slip.'

'Good show!' Colonel Heather said. He turned the knife over thoughtfully. 'What do you think? A bloody handprint on the handle?'

'Why not?' Midge agreed. 'Pull out all the stops.'

'Right you are.' He dipped his hand into the blood, then let most of it roll off. 'They won't get any fingerprints from these rubber gloves—not that any of them would know what to do with a fingerprint if they had one.'

'I'm afraid some of them would try,' Midge said. 'And it would be a dead bore to get all inky and messy.'

'We'll make sure they realize that gloves were worn.' Colonel Heather grasped the handle firmly with his bloodied glove, then carefully released it. The effect was satisfactorily gory. 'Where do you want this now? On the floor or the bed?'

'The floor, I think. Grace is going to drape herself across the bed. Give them two focal points.'

'Like this?' Grace obligingly pitched forward, face down, her head lolling off the side of the bed. Her arm dangled over her head at an awkward, potentially painful, angle.

'Wait a minute.' She changed position. Now her arm lay twisted behind her on the bed, another position where it would begin to ache in a very short time. 'Oh—' Grace Holloway had discovered the actress's perennial problem— 'what do I do with my hands?'

'Just try it this way.' Midge eased the arm into a more

comfortable angle. 'You don't have to stay like that right now. Just remember the way you are and fall back into it when you hear me leading the guests up to discover you. I'll make enough noise to warn you.'

'All right.' Grace sat up, rubbing her arm. 'There's more to it than there looks, isn't there?'

There was a sharp rap on the door. Grace gasped and hurled herself across the bed again. Colonel Heather stepped back out of the line of vision as Midge cautiously opened the door.

'Right.' Eric stepped briskly into the room. 'I think I've got it now.' His gaze fell on Grace and he shuddered visibly. 'Oh my God! That's grotesque!'

'It's supposed to be.' Midge turned him around and opened the door again. 'Let's go downstairs and announce that we've just found her body.'

Grace sat up, blood oozing from her cardigan and dripping on the counterpane. 'Don't be long. Hermione was right—this stuff gets cold and clammy. It's like sitting around in a wet bathing suit.'

'We'll be no time at all,' Midge assured her, shepherding Eric and Colonel Heather out into the corridor. 'Remember, keep your face turned away and don't move. I'll shuffle them in and out as fast as possible.' She closed the door behind them.

'I'm sorry,' Eric said, trailing them down the corridor, 'but I think all that blood is in very bad taste. I'm surprised Miss Holloway allows it. Why can't she be a tidy discreet corpse, like the other one?'

Midge and Colonel Heather exchanged one startled, uncomprehending glance, then swung around to face Eric.

'What other one?' Midge asked.

'The one I nearly tripped over at the foot of the service stairs—the crazy one. Now she looked quite respectable. Scarcely any blood at all. Of course, the knife was still in the wound—I've heard that makes a difference. But need you be so graphic with Miss Holloway? She's far more ladylike than the other one—I'm surprised she didn't object.'

'The other one,' Midge repeated faintly. She and Colonel Heather wheeled and raced for the service stairs. The Colonel reached up and pressed the switch hidden in the candle sconce, the concealed panel swung open.

'I say—' Eric brought up the rear. 'What's biting you two?' He followed them down the stairs.

She was lying at the foot of the stairs, just inside the ground-floor secret panel. As Eric had said, she looked quite tidy and discreet. As he had failed to notice, she also looked extremely dead.

'Is there a pulse?' Colonel Heather asked without hope, fumbling for the limp wrist. 'No,' he answered himself. 'Not a flutter.'

'I say—' Eric was uncertain now, looking from one to the other. 'What's the—?'

'*Whe-eew*—' The whistle came from above. 'So that explains our ghostly noises. Secret passages!' Bertha Stout came into view, behind her was Stanley Marric.

'Oh no,' Midge moaned. 'We left the panel open.'

'What's going on down here?' Bertha asked eagerly. 'Is that a body? Who got it this time?'

'I don't know.' Eric seemed the only one able to speak. 'But she does it awfully well.'

'Hey!' Bertha moved closer and peered down at the body. 'That's one of the Chandlers. Leave it to them,' she said in disgust, 'to try to get in on the act.'

'She—She's not act—' Midge's voice evaporated in a squeak. She swallowed helplessly.

Over her head, Colonel Heather met Stanley Marric's eyes and slowly shook his head.

'Dead? Dead?' Bertha was incredulous. 'She can't be. She —Which one is it?'

Midge still stood frozen, all the implications bursting upon her. The others hadn't got that far yet.

'Her name tag says "Brigid",' Colonel Heather stooped

again and reported. 'But you can't go by that. I suspect they were always switching them back and forth.'

'They did it all the time,' Bertha agreed. 'They thought it was terribly funny.'

'The other one is going to take it hard,' Stan said uneasily. 'I mean, a twin—'

'God, yes!' Bertha was plunged into gloom, the implications were filtering through to her, too. 'If you ask me, neither of them was too stable. They had more money than brains—and that wouldn't have been hard.'

'We'd better let Roberta tell the other one.' Stan's brow cleared slightly as he saw the unpleasant task could be delegated. 'She knew them both better than any of us.'

'Good thing she's here.' Bertha was in complete agreement. 'If she hadn't made it before the blizzard cut us off—'

'That's right,' Colonel Heather said softly. 'The problem is trickier than it looks at first sight, isn't it?'

'Hell!' Bertha said decisively. 'We've got to call in the cops!'

'We'll do that now.' Midge regained her voice. 'If you'll just step outside and wait for me, I'll go upstairs and lock the panel so that no one else can stumble into the passage. We—we'll have to leave everything as it is, so that the police can see it.' The police could get through, couldn't they? If they couldn't make it by road, they had helicopters—

'I'll take care of the upstairs panel,' Colonel Heather said. 'You'd better find Reggie and let him know what's happened. Then call the police.'

'Reggie—' Midge stumbled towards the exit, heedless of whether the others were following her. She wanted Reggie. She wanted to collapse into his arms and let him take over. Behind her, she was dimly aware of the click of the lock, securing the hidden panel against accidental discovery.

'That this should happen,' Eric muttered, 'in *my* home.'

Of them all, Colonel Heather was the only one who remembered Miss Holloway. After locking the upstairs panel from the outside, he went back to her room, tapped on the door and entered.

She lay almost motionless. The bed was still quivering from the force with which she had thrown herself across it—trying not to giggle—waiting for the first shrieks of horror.

'You can get up now, Grace. The game is over.' Colonel Heather sighed deeply. 'They've started killing each other, instead.'

CHAPTER 14

The comfort Reggie provided was warm, but too brief. A hug, a quick kiss, then he broke away. 'I'll take a look myself. You can't be sure. Perhaps she's still alive—there may be something we can do.'

'There isn't—' Midge began, but he was gone. Roberta Rinehart hurried after him, a haunted look on her face.

'You've had a nasty shock—' Cook rallied round with restoratives. 'You'd all best have a drop of the cooking brandy.' She brought out a bottle from the depths of a cupboard.

'Good God!' Eric went ashen as he saw the label. 'You're not using that for cooking? It's my rarest cognac—it's eighty years old.'

'Time it was used, then.' Cook poured briskly. 'Doesn't do any good lying around in the cellar going stale—and it burns a treat on the plum puddings.'

'Don't waste any!' Eric cried in agony as drops fell to the table-top between glasses. 'Here, let me do that.' He took the bottle from her and poured reverently—and not so generously.

Ackroyd, obeying the injunction against waste, quietly leaped on to the table and began lapping up the lost drops.

'That isn't very sanitary.' Bertha stroked him absently. 'But I don't blame you. This is very good brandy.'

'It ought to be,' Eric said bitterly. 'How much is left in the cellar?'

'I'm sure I don't know.' Cook tossed her head. 'I have more important things to think about.'

'So have we.' Midge called them back to order. 'We must—' She broke off and took another sip of cognac. It didn't bear thinking about. The police . . . an undertaker —or did the police take care of that? And didn't the American Embassy have to be notified of the death of a citizen?

'Steady on.' With a faintly martyred air, Eric poured more of his precious cognac into her glass.

'That's not a bad idea.' Stan held out his glass. Bertha did likewise. Eric gritted his teeth and vouchsafed them a few more drops.

'Jeez, can you spare it?' Stan stared at the barely perceptible rise in the level of his drink. 'It's only booze, you know. You didn't have to open a vein.'

'*Please!*' Midge shuddered.

'Ooops, sorry. I wasn't thinking.'

'All right, all right.' Eric tilted the bottle over Stan's glass again. This time, the result was satisfactory.

'Don't be a chauvinist.' Bertha thrust her glass forward. Eric obliged grudgingly.

'What I want to know,' Cook said, 'is, do we serve tea now? I've got to get that out of the way before I can start on the Gala Dinner. I've got a Baron of Beef to roast.'

Midge jumped involuntarily as the kitchen door was flung open, but it was only Reggie.

'You were right,' he said. 'She *is* dead.'

'Sure she is,' Stan said. 'We wouldn't make a mistake about a thing like that.'

'No.' Reggie snatched the brandy from his father and poured with a reckless hand.

'Be careful,' Eric pleaded. 'That's liquid gold.'

'I'll have to ring the police.' Reggie set down the empty glass.

'You can ring them,' Bertha said, 'but are they going to be able to get here through all that?' She gestured to the falling snow. 'It hasn't let up all day and the radio was saying the roads were impassable hours ago.'

'That's their problem.' Reggie lifted the receiver. 'Our duty is to report this as soon as possible.'

'Where's Roberta?' Midge suddenly missed her.

'She's gone to find Lauren.' Reggie did not look up from dialling.

A long harrowing scream sounded from somewhere above.

'I guess she found her,' Stan said.

'Damn!' Reggie broke the connection and began dialling again. 'I'm not getting through.'

'Probably the overhead wires are down,' Bertha said. 'It always happens in a blizzard.'

'We don't have overhead wires,' Reggie frowned at the unresponsive phone. 'Our lines are carried by underground cable.'

'That phone was always quirky,' Cook said. 'Sometimes it cuts right out when I'm ordering from the tradesmen. That's why we get such strange deliveries sometimes.'

'I'll try the one in the office.' Reggie started for the door, the others trailing after him. Everyone but his father, who was heading in the opposite direction, and Cook, who had returned to her saucepans.

'Aren't you coming, Eric?' Midge asked.

'No, I'm going down to the cellar,' Eric said with icy bitterness. 'I want to check the inventory.'

'He's awfully nosey about poor Sir Cedric's wine cellar,' Stan told Reggie. 'I'd keep my eye on him, if I were you.'

Eric slammed the door behind him violently.

They walked into hopeful chaos in the lobby.

'Who screamed?'

'What's happened now?'

'I'll bet Miss Holloway got it—she knew too much.'

'Naw, it'll be somebody you don't expect—maybe Lettie. She's got more going than anybody admits.'

Reggie stalked grim-faced through their midst, ignoring all attempts to question him. Bertha and Stan dropped behind to spread the news. As Midge closed the office door, she heard the first gasps of astonishment, even indignation.

'Brigid? But she's one of *us*. She shouldn't be part of the game. How did she get into it?'

'It's not part of the game,' Bertha said with grim relish. 'She's really dead. They're calling the cops now.'

Midge closed the office door firmly and leaned against it, suddenly weak at the knees again. How were the police going to react when they learned about the game? She had the uneasy feeling that they would not appreciate it.

At the desk, Reggie shook the receiver, clicked the cradle and pawed desperately at the dial. 'It's no use,' he admitted finally. 'This one's dead, too. I'm afraid they all are.'

'But it's an underground cable.' Midge clung weakly to the one fact she was sure of. 'Unless it does go into overhead wires somewhere near the Exchange.'

'Or else—' Reggie was following the telephone line around the wainscotting to the point at which it was introduced into the house from outside the window. The level of snow on the window-ledge was uneven, as though it had been disturbed at some point during the storm. Reggie opened the window and leaned out. His face was grim as he moved back and closed the window again.

'It's been cut.'

'Oh no! Can't you splice it together or something?'

'It's not a straight cut. There's about a two-inch section missing entirely. Someone doesn't want us in touch with the outside world. We're marooned here until the snow stops and the roads are open again.'

'That could be days!' Midge stared hopelessly at the

leaden sky, the relentlessly falling snow. 'What are we going to do?'

'We're going to be very careful—' Reggie looked towards the closed door and his face changed. 'The problem now is —' he began tiptoeing towards the door—'we can't leave the body lying in the passageway until the police arrive. God knows when that will be. We'll have to move it to a cooler place.'

Midge winced. 'The toolshed?' she suggested tentatively. Then, as he motioned to her to continue talking, 'If you can get to it, that is. Otherwise, I suppose we might put her in—'

Reggie's hand was on the doorknob now, turning it silently. She faltered and continued, 'Put her in the back—'

'Come in!' Reggie pulled open the door and Haila Bond fell into the room. 'I hope we were talking loudly enough for you,' he said with dangerous courtesy.

'Not quite.' She got to her feet cheerfully and brushed her skirt. 'But I got most of it.' She turned and informed the others huddled in the doorway behind her. 'Someone's cut the telephone line, so we can't call the cops.'

'Aaah . . .' There was a murmur of gratification rather than surprise. This was just what they had expected.

'If we're going to move the body,' Haila informed Reggie briskly, 'we'd better take some photographs of it *in situ*. The cops will want to know how it was. I'll lend you my Polaroid. There's a new deck of film in it.'

'Good thinking!' someone applauded from the doorway.

'I'll bring down my Polaroid, too,' Asey said. 'We'll want lots of shots from every angle.'

'And mine,' someone else contributed. 'You can't have too many pictures.'

There was something wrong about their attitudes. After a moment, Midge realized what. 'Reggie,' she said faintly, 'Reggie, they don't believe it. They think it's part of the performance.'

'Of course it is.' Lauren spoke from the doorway. 'It has to be. It can't possibly be true.'

Behind her, Roberta spread her hands in a gesture of helplessness and shook her head.

'I don't know how you talked Brigid into doing it without letting me know,' Lauren said. 'She can't have thought it through. She'll have to be left out of everything now. It will ruin the whole weekend for her. But she's pretty dumb sometimes—she just has to learn the hard way.'

'I'm sorry—' Roberta shook her head again, looking dazed. 'She screamed and I thought she realized—But then she said it was impossible and she won't be convinced. I just don't know how to handle this.'

'It's all too silly.' Lauren's smile was bright and glazed, she looked over their heads. 'Where's Bramwell? He'll make her stop all this nonsense.'

'This is going to take shock tactics,' Bertha said. 'There's only one way she's going to believe it. You'll have to show her the body.'

'Yes . . . yes . . .' The cry was taken up by the others. 'Let's see the body. Where is it?'

'No,' Reggie said. 'Perhaps Lauren will have to view the body—but no one else. It isn't a peepshow.'

They faced him stubbornly. That was why they were here. They had paid—and far more than a pin—to see the peepshow.

'You bet I want to view the "body",' Lauren said. 'I'll shake some sense into her.'

'That's right,' someone said. 'She's throwing the whole game off, pushing herself into the middle like this.'

Midge moved closer to Reggie and exchanged a despairing look with him. It was no use. They weren't going to believe it until . . .

'All right.' Reggie gave in abruptly. 'Get your cameras and come along. We'll have to move her, anyway.'

The actors brought up the rear, looking strangely formless

and dispossessed, their roles usurped by actual life—and death. They were not only uneasy, they were frightened. They kept together in a defensive group as they walked behind the guests.

Reggie was leading the way to the secret panel and, catching the mood from the actors, Midge was suddenly afraid for him. His back was so unprotected. She moved closer to him.

'Oooh! . . . Aaah! . . . A secret passage.'

'Of course, there *had* to be one.'

'That's how come Petronella's father was popping in and out like a ghost.'

The appreciative chorus rose into a gratified hubbub. This was coming up to their expectations. The trouble was that it compounded the unreality. They still didn't believe anyone was truly dead. Not even when they viewed the body.

'Hey, look at that!'

'I didn't know she could act.'

'You're doing a great job, kid!'

'Stand back, let me get her in the viewfinder.'

'Get up, you fool!' Her twin strode forward and bent to shake her.

'Hold it—' Reggie caught her hand. 'Let them get their picture before you touch her. The police are likely to be upset enough because we're moving the body, but we can't leave it here.'

'I should think not!' Lauren stepped back and eyed her twin with disfavour. 'She'll catch her death of cold lying on that icy linoleum—and serve her right!'

'Gee, she's awfully still . . .' Those crowded at the front were beginning to feel the first qualms as they stared down at the body. They shuffled aside uneasily while those at the back pushed forward. The sporadic brilliance of flash bulbs set them blinking.

'I don't like this any more—' A normally quiet guest spoke in the tones of one about to ask for her money back.

They had paid to step into a fantasy, but now . . . 'It's . . . it's too . . . gruesome. Let's go get our tea.'

The escapists moved away, still believing that they could put it all behind them. Midge only wished that it were possible.

'I hate to say this—' Dixon Carr was the first to voice the growing suspicion—'but I don't think they're kidding. I'm afraid she really *is* dead.'

'We told you so,' Bertha Stout said. 'You might have believed us.'

Slowly, the cameras were lowered. Foreboding glances were slanted towards Lauren. She had denied the truth already; could she maintain the self-deception with her sister's body lying at her feet?

'Let me go!' Lauren tore herself free of Reggie's restraining grip. 'Brigid!' she screamed. 'Get up!'

The motionless form remained motionless.

'Get up! Get up! Get up!' Lauren hurled herself at her sister. This time, no one moved to stop her. She grabbed the limp shoulders, then froze.

They watched as realization seeped into her consciousness, reaching her through the very inertness of the shoulders beneath her hands.

The blankness of shock blotted all expression from her face. She withdrew her hands and backed away, whimpering.

'I'm sorry—' Roberta began.

'She's dead . . .' Lauren stared incredulously at the blood on her hands. 'Dead. My sister . . . my twin . . . *me*. The other half of *me* . . . murdered.'

Instinctively, everyone moved back as she turned slowly to confront them. The actors had retreated so far they were almost out of sight, although not out of earshot.

'Who did it?' Lauren demanded of the tour members, the people who had been in deadly proximity for the past ten days. 'Who killed us?'

CHAPTER 15

Ackroyd stalked the kitchen, twitching and purring as the rich aroma of roasting beef perfumed his air.

'I never did hold with all this,' Cook told him, crashing another pan into the sink. 'And now look where it's got us. Bodies—real live bodies—dead all over my outside storehouse.'

Ackroyd twined himself around her ankles, assuring her of complete agreement.

'Cupboard love,' she accused, freeing her ankles. 'You'd agree with anyone who could open the fridge or cooker.'

'Don't forget working tin-openers. They also loom large in his young life.' Midge entered and slumped wearily into a chair. 'Where is everyone?'

'I don't know—and I'm sure I don't care.'

'I don't mean the guests. I know where they are. They're all in their rooms dressing for dinner.'

Cook sniffed.

'They might as well,' Midge defended. 'They have to eat, anyway. "Business as usual" is a better attitude than screaming panic.'

'Call that business!' Cook said. 'How they can sit down and eat with each other, knowing one of themselves is a murderer, I can't imagine.'

'Perhaps they haven't got that far yet,' Midge said. 'Perhaps they think one of *us* did it.'

'Oh, good—' Cedric poked his head cautiously around the door, then advanced into the kitchen. 'The coast is clear. Hermione is just coming. She's making sure her tiara is on straight.'

'I don't like it,' Cook said. 'I wish you didn't have to go out there again tonight.'

'I don't,' Cedric said. 'I'm safely dead. But I know what

you mean. I'd as soon Hermione stayed behind the scenes where it's safe. Still,' he added cheerfully, 'once she's murdered, she'll be all right.'

'You're not still going on with *that*.' Cook was shocked.

'If we don't, there's going to be a long, dour evening ahead, with everyone sitting around brooding and suspecting each other.'

'And quite rightly,' Cook said. 'One of them did it.'

'We don't want them to start thinking about that,' Midge pointed out. 'It's much safer to keep them concentrating on imaginary murders. If they decide to try to track down the real killer, they could be in deadly danger. We must do all we can to keep the surface smooth until the police can take over—and heaven knows when that will be.'

'Where's Reggie?' Cedric asked abruptly. 'He hasn't gone out in this to try to fetch them, has he?'

'He's not that foolhardy. The temperature has been dropping by the minute ever since it began to get dark.'

A discreet tap sounded from the kitchen entrance to the servants' passage, the panel moved and Miss Holloway fluttered into the room, followed by Colonel Heather. 'I do hope this is in order,' she said. 'We . . . we didn't want to Make Our Entrance until we discovered which way the wind was blowing.'

'Quite so,' the Colonel said. 'We mean, is this the sort of Show that Must Go On? We're not cancelling out, are we?'

'There's no danger of that, is there?' Hermione had appeared in the doorway in time to hear the question. 'I'm sure we ought to go on but, in view of what's happened, I don't think I should be stabbed. It would not only be bad taste but, for all we know, someone might get over-excited at the sight of blood. I don't think we should risk it.'

'Quite right,' Cedric said. 'I must say, I don't like the idea of knives around Hermione myself. Can't you switch the method to poison instead? Cut the risk of one of those bleeders going berserk with blood-lust or whatever.'

'That should be easy enough, ' Midge agreed. 'We've

already planted doubts about the cocktails. We'll fall back on the cyanide gimmick. Hermione can keel over after an injudicious drink.'

'Before dinner?' Cedric asked hopefully.

'It had better be after,' Midge decided. 'We'll want to see what the prevailing feeling is before we go too far. If they have strong objections, we'll have to cancel the rest of the performance, but most of them seemed anxious for the weekend to continue as scheduled.'

'Just the same—' Cedric threw an arm around his wife's shoulders and drew her to him in a rare display of affection. 'Watch yourself, old girl. I don't like your being out there among those nutters without me to keep an eye on you.'

'I'll be all right.' Hermione re-settled her tiara with a gratified air. 'It was obviously a personal thing. Someone settling a private score.'

'Who?' The question slipped out before Midge could stop it; she had promised herself that she wasn't going to think about that tonight.

'Practically anyone, I should imagine,' Cedric said, not very helpfully. 'That was a most tedious young woman. Neither she nor her twin would be much missed.'

'Damnably difficult, twins.' Colonel Heather was equally unhelpful. 'Question is, did they get the right one? Or do they mean to get both of them before they're done?'

'Please!' Midge wailed. 'Don't even suggest such a thing. It doesn't bear thinking about.'

'Hiding your head in the sand won't do any good,' Cedric said. 'Jack's got a sound point there. How do we know they've finished? We haven't.'

'That's another thing,' Miss Holloway said, as Midge began to feel reality slide away from her. 'What happens to me now? I mean, am I still going to be murdered? Or is it just Hermione? I've lost track.'

'Just me,' Hermione said firmly. 'We're back to the original script.'

'In that case, what am I to do?' Miss Holloway looked

distressed. 'I spent all tea-time promising them a Startling Revelation after dinner. And now I'm still alive and I haven't any idea what I can tell them.'

'Oh Lord,' Midge said. 'I'd forgotten that.'

'Ha—she's got you there,' Cedric crowed. 'You're going to have to come up with something.'

'Let me think about it,' Midge said. 'I'll talk to Reggie—'

'String it out until my death scene,' Hermione suggested practically. 'Tell them you can't speak while I'm around. Act afraid of me. Then, after I'm murdered, you'll be another strong suspect.'

'What a splendid idea!' Grace Holloway exclaimed with delight. I shall—'

The sharp peal of the bell startled them all. The familiar number swung mockingly in its box.

'Bramwell and I will require dinner in our rooms tonight,' Amaryllis said regally.

'I'm sorry, Mrs Barbour, that won't be possible.'

'Not possible?' Amaryllis drew herself up. 'Surely you must understand that what has happened changes everything. My son cannot possibly be expected to expose himself to the company of murderers—'

'Mrs Barbour, even with the best will in the world—' something in Midge's tone warned Amaryllis that this was not being extended—'what you suggest would be impossible. We're desperately short-handed. The storm has cut us off, the girls can't get through from the village—'

'Nonsense!' Amaryllis said. 'It stopped snowing an hour ago.'

Midge went to the window to check. She pulled back the curtain and gazed out on a spotless snow-shrouded landscape. A waxing moon hung in a cloudless black sky, casting strange shadows on terrain made unfamiliar by deep white drifts.

'Even so—' Midge turned back into the room. 'Snow

ploughs will have to clear the roads before anyone can get through. It could be twenty-four hours, perhaps longer, before they get to us. No one is going to come from the village tonight. I shall have to ask you and Bramwell to take your places in the dining-room, as usual.'

'That's monstrous!' Amaryllis's voice rose. 'You are deliberately putting our lives in danger. I have a good mind to —to leave at once!'

'If you think you can—' Midge abandoned tact—'go ahead.'

'It's all right, Midge.' Bramwell had opened his door quietly and come into the sitting-room. 'Mother's just upset. She doesn't mean what she's saying. We'll be down for dinner.'

The atmosphere was neutral and guarded as the meal commenced. The guests noticed, but refrained from commenting upon, the fact that one of the two places at the Chandler twins' table had been removed and the ranks closed. The other place had been taken by Eric.

Tentatively, the polite conversations began, opened by the actor at each table. Reggie had chosen the most powerful wine and kept the glasses topped up so that the guests lost track of the amount they were drinking.

Gradually the tension eased. Someone dared to ask how Lauren was . . . where she was?

'Sleeping,' Midge said shortly. 'We gave her a couple of sleeping pills. She'll be out until morning.'

They relaxed still more after that. They began to feel their way back into the original purpose of the weekend. A few pointed questions were asked, unfortunately, of the wrong people.

'Do you still feel guilty over your wife's death?'

'Me?' Eric was understandably startled. 'Guilty? Why should I?'

'Well, you *were* driving, weren't you?'

'Was I?' Eric looked around for help. Midge realized this

was a plot point she had neglected to warn him about.

'Please—' Petronella leaned over from her table to rescue him. 'Don't upset Daddy. He hates remembering. Sometimes he can't. The doctors called it selective amnesia.'

'Very convenient,' someone said and there was a murmur of assent. They were getting back on the trail.

Midge cleared the soup plates and carried them back to the kitchen where Cedric was helping Cook carve and serve up. Fluffy golden Yorkshire puddings floated on seas of gravy and roast potatoes nestled beside mounds of succulent beef. Midge began ladling pearl onions and peas into any available space on the plates. Without any help, it was easier to do everything in the kitchen rather than try to cope with serving dishes. Reggie loaded a tray with the filled plates and staggered into the dining-room.

The rest of them continued filling plates while Reggie and Lettie returned at brisk intervals to reload their trays. Midge had lost count of the servings when Cook said, 'There, that's the last one. Tell them they can have seconds, if they like. There's plenty left.'

Midge loaded the last few plates on to a tray of her own and brought it into the dining-room. Fortunately, the last table to be served was so deep in conversation no one had minded waiting.

'Ah, our charming housekeeper—' Dixon Carr leaned to one side as Midge slid his plate in front of him. 'Surely the person we should compliment on the marvellous re-creation of the Golden Age.'

'Golden for whom?' Bertha Stout challenged. 'Have you read those books? Really read them?'

'Of course I have. What do you mean by that?'

'You can't have, or you'd know what I mean. Unless you read them without thinking, you must be totally uncritical.'

'I wouldn't say that. I've always prided myself that I'm as good a critic as the next man—or woman.'

'And you can still call it the Golden Age? Oh, I've read most of them and, believe me, I approach them as though they're a hand grenade with the pin out. You never know when they're going to blow up in your face. You're reading along and everything is drowsy afternoon, old lace, the hum of bees in the hollyhocks, church bells chiming the hour and honey for tea when—Pow! Suddenly, you're rocked back on your heels by a blast of anti-Semitism that leaves you reeling. And it's so casual, so taken-for-granted. Perhaps that's the worst of all.'

'It was part of the climate of the times,' Dix agreed uneasily. 'Seen in historical perspective, it goes a long way towards explaining how Hitler got away with it in his push to power. The scapegoats were ready-made by the attitudes already in existence.'

'Right—so it wasn't so golden if you were Jewish. Then there's the attitude towards women. The gilt started wearing pretty thin on the gingerbread as the years wore on. If you were over twenty-two or so, you were over the hill. How many times have you been reading and—another Pow! You come across a description like: "There were still remnants of the great beauty she had had in her youth, although she must have been thirty-five at least." There's a sexism to warm the cockles of your heart.'

'It wasn't just against women,' Dix argued. 'It was ageism, plain and simple. You can fall over the description of a doddering old man making his Will before he's too senile to be able to make a valid distribution of his worldly goods. Then, a few pages later, he has a birthday party surrounded by his loving kin, waiting to see if he'll survive the excitement of the party—and you then discover he's all of sixty-two.'

'And, if you were a servant—forget it!' Bertha turned to check Lettie's whereabouts before continuing. 'Take Lettie now. She'd have started as a skivvy in a manor house like this when she was about twelve. Up at five in the morning, lighting fires, cleaning and blackleading the grates, carrying jugs of hot water to rooms, and most of the time scurrying around between the walls in that rabbit-run of a passage—'

'Ahem.' Dix cleared his throat loudly, reminding her that she was straying too close to the perilous reality of the present in her delineation of the unpleasant realities of the past.

'Yes, well . . .' Bertha veered sharply away from the dangerous corner. 'You can keep the Golden Age. Give me the Forties—they were writing them better then. Look at Craig Rice, Frances and Richard Lockridge, Cornell Woolrich—'

'Please—' Wincing, Dix held up his hand to stop her. Silence had fallen on the surrounding tables and he raised his voice. 'We needn't go so far back. It would be churlish to except present company. I give you a toast.' He rose and lifted his glass. 'To the writers of today. In particular, to our gracious host and hostess, who have given us so much reading pleasure. To Evelina T. Carterslee and Bramwell Barbour!'

They all pushed back their chairs and lurched to their feet, repeating the names and waving their glasses in the air. Evelina and Bramwell remained seated, eyes modestly downcast.

Only Amaryllis Barbour seemed unhappy with the toast. She glanced around restlessly, as though she felt something were missing from it. Herself, perhaps. She was facing the doorway and suddenly she stiffened.

'Oh no!' she gasped.

Bramwell, rising to respond to the toast, followed his mother's gaze and choked. One by one, the others turned, their hilarity spluttering into silence.

'Well—' Lauren Chandler advanced into the dining-room, pouting. 'I don't think it was very polite of you to start the party without us.'

'Miss Chandler—' Reggie was the first to recover; he hurried to her side. 'Are you feeling better?'

'Oh yes.' She looked at him vaguely. 'My headache is all gone, so we decided to come down. We'd hate to miss anything. Has there been another murder yet?'

Someone caught his breath audibly, a woman half-sobbed. Lauren regarded the staring faces with mild disapproval.

'We're just serving dinner.' Reggie looked towards Midge for support. 'Let me find you a seat—'

'Come and sit here, Lauren.' Stanley Marric crowded his chair into Algie's, causing a hasty reshuffle at his table. 'Reggie will bring a chair.'

'I'm not Lauren.' She looked at him coldly. 'I'm Brigid.'

'Then you *had* switched name tags again,' Haila Bond said. 'Just as we suspected. It's really Lauren who's lying out there—' She broke off abruptly, flushing.

'I don't know what you're talking about.' The voice was colder than ever. '*I'm* Lauren.'

'Holy Jeez!' Marric said. 'She's flipped!'

CHAPTER 16

Lauren-Brigid demanded two bowls of soup and finished both of them. When she insisted on two dinners, Midge, worrying about emergency first aid for stomach upsets, produced drastically reduced portions. The twin did not appear to notice and, fortunately, seemed content with one chair. There was no denying that she cast a pall over the entire assembly.

By the time everyone retired to the drawing-room for coffee, Hermione had developed a bad case of stage fright. Not without reason.

'I don't think I can do it,' she said, watching Reggie smoothly set two demi-tasse cups beside Lauren-Brigid. 'Not with her watching. I'm afraid to. What if it pushes her over the edge?'

'Hrrmph!' Colonel Heather snorted. 'Shouldn't think there was an edge left for her to go over.'

'I'm afraid Colonel Heather is right, dear,' Grace Holloway said. 'It would be hard to see how she could get any worse. The best thing to do, surely, is to carry on and give her something to occupy her mind.'

'Both of 'em.' Colonel Heather seemed on the verge of amusement. Miss Holloway gave him a withering look.

'Here.' Midge carried a brandy over from the bar for Hermione. 'Have this and take it easy for a bit. You don't have to do anything right away. The actors are going ahead as scheduled. You can keep in the background until it's your turn.'

Lettie wheeled in the coffee urn. Ivor Novello sang of Ruritanian romance. A soothing air of unreality settled over the assemblage.

Except for a marked disinclination to address the remaining Chandler by any name whatsoever, everything was much the same as it had been last night.

'So far, so good,' Reggie murmured, as the Hon. Petronella took the floor with Algie for a foxtrot.

'I'm not going to uncross my fingers until we get away from here,' Roberta said. 'If we do. What will happen when the police come? Will they let us go—or will they want to keep us in the country as material witnesses?'

'I don't know—' Reggie began.

'If you don't, who does?' Dix and the Dains had come up behind them. 'With all your experience at Scotland Yard, you should have some idea of the correct procedures.'

'That's right,' Alice Dain said. 'Thank heavens we have you here. I'd feel so frightened without you. You're going to take over, aren't you, and have the whole case solved by the time the police arrive?'

'But I—' Reggie broke off as he was simultaneously kicked in the shins by both Midge and Roberta. 'I really have retired from the Yard,' he ended weakly.

'Nonsense,' Dix said. 'Once a Scotland Yard man, always a Scotland Yard man. We're depending on you.'

Edwin Lupin moved over to the dancing couple and cut in on Algie, who relinquished the Hon. Pet reluctantly in response to the tap on his shoulder and stood disconsolately looking around. Then, with sudden purpose, he moved across the room, bowed to Lauren-Brigid and led her out on the floor.

'Look at that!' Alice Dain gasped. 'That—that fortune-hunter is after poor ... er, uh ... now. He's lining up another heiress in case Petronella comes to her senses.'

'That's right,' Norman Dain said. 'And, with her sister gone, she'll have all the money and no one to argue over how she spends it. Leave it to *him* to think of that!'

Amaryllis appeared to be thinking about that, too. She pushed at Bramwell's elbow, obviously urging him to a course of action he was reluctant to take.

'I wouldn't put it past Algie to have killed poor ... whichever-it-was himself—' Alice continued making out her case. 'Everybody knows a bereaved twin is a pushover for the first man who comes along—unless she dies of grief before she can form another attachment. Grief—or maybe gets murdered herself.'

'Don't talk like that, honey.' Norman tried to restrain his wife. 'Who'd want to murder her?'

'Who wanted to murder the other one?'

'The real question is: *cui bono?*' Dix was watching thoughtfully as Bramwell shook off his mother's hand and retreated to a corner, joining Miss Holloway and Colonel Heather. 'Who benefits?'

'Bramwell would get them both off his back.' Alice Dain followed the lead eagerly. 'Also his mother, if neither of them were around. Of course, that would also be true if the Chandler twin were to marry someone else—like Algie.'

'Do you really think she might?' Norman looked at the couple, who were dancing without enjoyment. Lauren-Brigid's face was sulky. Whatever Algie was saying to her was not getting a particularly enthusiastic reception.

'Why shouldn't she? She must know Bramwell isn't keen on her. Who else has she got?'

Someone had changed the record on the gramophone and

Noel Coward was now conducting an interrogation of his own:

> 'What is there to strive for,
> Love or keep alive for? . . .'

Reggie shuddered and moved away.

'Are you going to begin the questioning?' Alice asked eagerly.

'No, I'm going to open the bar,' Reggie said. 'I don't know about the rest of you, but I could use a drink.'

The Hon. Pet and Algie quarrelled discreetly, but unmistakably. At one point, her voice was raised high enough so that everyone heard her say, 'After all I've done for you—'

Edwin Lupin was observed to lean threateningly over Miss Holloway, his Nice American Boy mask slipping, as she cringed with terror. Later, he appeared to have fallen out with Lady Hermione, who looked at him with regal disdain and pointedly moved to the far side of the drawing-room.

Eric, still bemused by the proceedings, had withdrawn to a corner of the bar with Colonel Heather and was deep in conversation, happily unaware that he was coming in for more than his share of the suspicion.

Lettie was assisting at the bar, taking orders from the guests scattered around the huge room and returning with their drinks on a tray. Several times she had unaccountably mixed up their orders and the guests were now viewing both her and their drinks with a certain uneasiness.

'Brrr . . .' Roberta drew back the drapes and stared out on a chill, bleak and silent white world. 'It's beautiful—yet so grim. I've never felt so cut off from the world before. At this point, I'd rather explain to everyone that the tour company has left us stranded than actually be stranded like this.'

'At least, the snow has stopped,' Midge said encouragingly. 'The world will begin moving again in the morning. The snow ploughs will be working all night to clear the roads.'

'And sooner or later the police will be able to get through.' Roberta let the drape fall back into place and turned away from the window with a sigh. 'I'm dreading that, too.'

'Unless they're already here.' Haila Bond and Stan Marric had come up behind them quietly.

Roberta started. 'What do you mean?'

'Just think a minute,' Haila said. 'Who was the last person to join the party? Unexpectedly. After Sir Cedric was murdered. Who came through the blizzard?'

'Like in *The Mousetrap*,' Stan prompted. 'The cop arriving on snowshoes when everybody thought the house was cut off.'

'Exactly.' Haila's eyes gleamed. 'Is he really a policeman? Or is he the murderer . . . trying a double bluff?'

'But he's Petronella's father,' Midge protested weakly. 'The tea planter from Ceylon.'

'So *she* says,' Haila said darkly. 'But how many of *you* have ever seen her real father? He's been out there for years, hasn't he? This one could be an impostor, maybe hired by Algie, to wipe out any opposition to the match.'

'And that would mean Pet was in on it, too. She's so besotted, she'd agree to anything.' Marric shook his head. 'I'm afraid I'm coming to the opinion that Ned Lupin ought to inherit.' He paused portentously. 'And I happen to know that the Chandler twins were coming round to the same opinion. And that's why Brigid, or whoever, got it!'

'But—' Midge felt reality lurch and begin slipping away from her.

'Oh, don't worry,' Marric said. 'I'll look out for myself. They're not going to catch *me* alone in any dark places. I'm not broadcasting my opinion, either. But it's got to be decided by tomorrow afternoon—and I know which way I'm voting.'

'I'm not so sure.' Haila glanced meaningly towards the large chair by the fire where Lauren-Brigid sat. Algie had just brought her two liqueurs and was hovering over her solicitously. In the background, Ned was gazing thoughtfully at the pair.

'If Pet is in cahoots with Algie and they've brought in this hit-man, I'd say she's backed the wrong horse. I don't like the way Algie has started paying so much attention to the Chandler dame. If you ask me, he's sighted richer pickings. Pet is going to find herself out in the cold—maybe with her neck in a noose.'

'That's a thought,' Midge said, without specifying where the thought was leading her. Ned had now moved over to offer Lauren-Brigid a plate of chocolate mints. Now both actors were paying more attention to one of the audience than to the supposed object of their affections.

Their motivation was clearer than any in the script. Their engagement in *Murder At the Manor* was ending with this weekend; they would soon be back in the West End, doing the weary rounds of agents and auditions. The lure of a wife or girlfriend rich enough to back a show all by herself was a powerful one. It was worth dancing attendance on someone so wealthy, even though her foibles included a difficult temperament and a split personality. An ambitious actor often had to put up with worse in the furtherance of his career.

Amaryllis appeared to be reaching the same conclusion. She glared at the group by the fire and crossed over to pull her son away from Colonel Heather and Miss Holloway. Once away, she spoke sharply to him. He did not move and she spoke again. He turned to look at Ned and Algie, just in time to see Lauren-Brigid simper up at them and sip at her liqueurs, first from the glass in one hand, then from the other.

A visible shudder shook him and he moved forward. Amaryllis's satisfied smile froze as he bypassed the group by the fire and went to join Evelina on the sofa. She moved aside to make room for him and patted his hand.

Both Amaryllis and Lettie glared at her.

'Just a cosy evening at the Old Manor,' Roberta murmured under her breath.

'Very cosy,' Midge agreed, busy with her own problems. Across the room, Lady Hermione was now in earnest discussion with Miss Holloway. Midge had a fairly good idea what they were arguing about. Hermione kept shaking her head. Miss Holloway was growing increasingly desperate. She looked at her watch. Hermione looked at Lauren-Brigid and shook her head again.

With a gesture of resignation, Miss Holloway returned to her chair, took up her knitting, and signalled to Lettie to bring her a drink.

Meanwhile, having missed the byplay, Reggie carried a liqueur glass of Amaretto over to Hermione and spoke to her urgently. Hermione stared at the glass with stubborn resentment.

The guests were growing restive. They had been airing their views and theories, but the initial impetus was running down. It was time for something else to happen before they began to grow bored. Worse, before their minds returned to nag at the real murder.

Someone stifled a yawn. There was a clicking cascade as Bertha Stout moodily demolished the house she had been constructing with the Mah Jong counters; she still hadn't cracked the rules of the game. Lauren-Brigid laughed a little too shrilly at something Algie said to her. In the background, Jessie Mathews mourned a lost love.

Miss Holloway gave one final despairing look around the room, then drained her glass and set it down with a decisive click. She took a deep breath and gave a choking gasp.

No one paid any attention. More drastic measures were necessary.

She lurched to her feet, clutched her throat and produced a strange mewling sound. She gave several convulsive movements of head and shoulders, then fell back into her chair and lay still.

Unfortunately, this was the same moment Hermione decided to heed the call of duty.

Too engrossed in her own impending performance to have noted Miss Holloway's preliminaries, Lady Hermione let her empty liqueur glass slip from her hand and roll across the floor. She sank to her knees, articulating a weak scream, then plunged face forward to lie sprawled across the carpet.

'Eeek!' . . . 'Oh no!' . . . 'Hey, look at that!'

Amid screams and cries of confusion, the guests divided into two groups, rushing to one body and then to the other.

'What happened?'

'Who was near them?'

'Don't let those glasses get away this time!'

'Oh, wow!' someone said gleefully. 'They both got it! Two of them at once. We never expected anything like this.'

'No,' Midge said faintly. 'Neither did we.'

CHAPTER 17

'Do you think it was a suicide pact?'

'Naw, never! Why would they do that? Look, they were fighting just a little while ago. More likely they tried to kill each other. And succeeded.'

'Maybe they died by accident. Maybe the whole bottle was poisoned, not just the glasses. Maybe it was left over from Sir Cedric's murder.'

'Different people brought them the drinks. Reggie gave Lady Hermione hers and Lettie served Miss Holloway.'

'That Lettie—she's been getting the drinks mixed up all evening. Maybe she took the wrong glass to Miss Holloway —it had been intended for Lady Hermione, then Reggie saw what she'd done and poured another dose of poison and brought it to Lady Hermione himself—to make sure there'd be no mistake.'

'But then wouldn't he have tried to stop Miss Holloway from drinking the poison?'

'Naw, he'd give himself away if he did. He wasn't supposed to know there was poison in the glass.'

'But it can't be Reggie—he's the Scotland Yard man!'

'Is he? Maybe he's Brutus, too.'

'Maybe Eric is. If Lady Hermione was an old friend of his, then he'd have known her brother, too. Another old friend.'

While the arguments raged around them, Eric and Colonel Heather solemnly advanced to fore and aft of Hermione, grasped her shoulders and feet firmly, heaved her aloft and bore her off swiftly.

Reggie signalled to Algie to come and help him with Miss Holloway, but Dix forestalled him.

'Allow me,' he said, taking her ankles. Reggie had no option but to let him assist, particularly as Algie seemed reluctant to move from Lauren-Brigid's side.

They negotiated the turn at the doorway a little more clumsily than might have been hoped. Dix was observing the conventions, however, and Miss Holloway's involuntary grimace was allowed to pass unremarked.

'This is terrible,' Dix said seriously. 'Terrible.'

'You're so right.' Reggie spoke a trifle grimly. It wasn't actually Miss Holloway's fault—she had meant well. It wasn't exactly Hermione's fault, either, she could not be blamed for her bout of stage fright. It was just highly unfortunate that they had both decided to take action at the same time.

'In here,' Midge said, opening the office door. It had been prearranged that the 'body' would be deposited in there. However, Eric and Colonel Heather had got there first and Lady Hermione was stretched out on the couch.

'Oh—perhaps not.' Reggie looked around desperately.

'The chair,' Midge suggested, tilting the reclining chair to its most horizontal position.

'Yes, fine.' Reggie and Dix arranged Miss Holloway on the chair. 'It will have to do,' Reggie said. Eric and Colonel Heather watched with interest. Hermione's eyelids twitched.

'I would like to extend my deepest sympathy—' Dix spoke in the formal tones of one addressing the next of kin. Eric jumped, then realized it wasn't meant for him.

'This is a terrible, terrible tragedy—' Dix looked directly at Colonel Heather—'after all the years it took you to get her to yourself at last.'

'Eh?' Colonel Heather said.

'You needn't pretend with me.' Dix patted him on the shoulder. 'I saw through your little ruse from the start. Don't worry, I won't tell the others.'

'I don't know what you're talking about.'

'You don't?' Dix gave a short, sharp laugh. 'I suppose the name Primrose means nothing to you?'

'Primrose? Primrose?' Colonel Heather looked at him wildly. 'Never knew a Primrose in my life. Knew a Poppy once—'

'Oh, you can play it that way if you like, but I *know*.'

'More than I do. Primrose path—?'

'Very clever. Not quite clever enough, though. You really shouldn't have let her keep the name Grace. I suppose Holloway was her maiden name?'

'Grace? Primrose?' Colonel Heather was lost.

'Did you make an honest woman of her? Or was this just a little fling? Not that your fans would think any the less of either of you in this day and age. We were always rooting for you two to get it together.'

'How dare you, sir!'

'Don't worry, your secret is safe with me. I'm just sorry it had to end this way.'

'Secret!' the Colonel spluttered. 'Damn it, man, there *is* no secret!'

'Aha, but there must be *one*.' Dix winked and nodded. 'What did you do with Sergeant Buck?'

'Buck? Buck?'

'It was over his dead body, wasn't it? Don't worry—' Dix winked again—'I'll never tell. We always thought he had it coming to him.' He patted Colonel Heather's shoulder again and left.

'Bonkers!' Colonel Heather stared after him incredulously. 'The man's stark staring bonkers!'

Midge returned to the drawing-room to make sure that all the guests were still safely assembled there. She signalled to Reggie that it was clear for Hermione and Grace to slip away to their own rooms, then stood guard in the doorway until they had had time to get away. Not that anyone appeared anxious to leave, the would-be sleuths were all too occupied with the new murders.

Lettie was at bay in a corner, Bertha Stout leading the pack that had converged on her. There were so many questions being shot at her that she couldn't even sort them out. She stood there, back pressed against the wall, shaking her head.

'I don't know.' There was genuine desperation in her voice. 'Honestly, I don't know anything about it.'

'You were serving drinks all evening.' Bertha was relentless. 'Surely you must remember who ordered what.'

'Why should she? She couldn't remember for five minutes, even then. She kept mixing up the orders all night.' Asey Wentworth slanted his eyes at her craftily. 'Were you really that dumb all of a sudden, Lettie? Or were you setting up an alibi?'

'I don't know why you're picking on me,' Lettie said. 'Everyone knows Miss Holloway had a weak heart. This weekend has been a tremendous strain on her. She must have had a heart attack and keeled over. It was natural causes.'

'And how about Lady Hermione?' Bertha sneered. 'I suppose she had a weak heart, too?'

'I—I d-don't know a-about that—' Lettie stammered, managing to look inexpressibly guilty. 'Lady Hermione d-did not confide in me.'

'I'll bet she didn't! She hated you, didn't she? And you hated her!'

'No!' Lettie spotted a break in their ranks and charged through it. 'It's no business of yours. Leave me alone!'

Midge stepped aside, nodding that the coast was clear, and Lettie ran through the lobby and up the main staircase. Several keen sleuths pursued her, but Bertha Stout bowed to her own weight and that of gravity and turned her attention elsewhere.

The Honourable Petronella, badgered and beleaguered by her own set of questioners, had dragged Algie away from his proposed conquest and grappled him firmly to her side. They now faced the music together.

'Who is Lady Hermione's heir—or heiress?' Haila Bond asked suspiciously.

'How should I know? It wouldn't be me. I didn't know her all that well. She was just doing Daddy a favour by seeing me through the Season.'

'Oh yes, your Daddy. A friend of hers. A very old friend, I believe. How much does he stand to inherit?'

'Probably nothing.' Petronella tightened her grip on Algie's arm as he tried to slide away. 'They weren't that close—not for a long time. Why don't you ask him?'

'Where is he? He helped carry the body off—and he hasn't come back.'

'I don't know any more than you do. I've been right here all the time.'

'Why hasn't he come back?' A couple on the fringe of the group moved away. 'Let's go find him.'

'The party's breaking up—' Ned, momentarily devalued as a top suspect, came over to stand beside Midge uneasily.

'Some of them are going off by themselves. Do you think it's safe?'

'I wish I knew.' The actors were now more suspicious of their audience, Midge realized, than the audience of the actors. And with far better reason. Someone in the audience was playing for keeps.

Perhaps it was not so surprising that Ned was having second thoughts and had moved away from Lauren-Brigid. Or had Amaryllis driven him away? She had taken his place beside Lauren-Brigid, bringing Bramwell with her. He was obviously unhappy about it, but he was there. It was equally obvious that his mother had no intention of letting him get away again.

Small groups around the room discussed theories amongst themselves, looking from one suspect to another, trying to decide which to approach and what leading questions to ask them.

Dix stood alone, still nodding in apparent self-congratulation at what he considered his discovery of Colonel Heather's secret life.

Evelina T. Carterslee sat in a corner in earnest discussion with Roberta Rinehart.

'Bit stuffy in here, isn't it?' Ned dabbed at his forehead with an initialled handkerchief.

'I could do with a breath of air,' Midge admitted. They slipped away unobtrusively, almost tiptoeing through the lobby to the front door.

The air was clear and arctic. They looked out at a glittering white world, sculptured by blue-black shadows, dotted with skeletal trees.

Midge strained her ears for the comforting sound of snow ploughs in the distance, but they were suspended in a silent world.

'Brr—' Ned stepped back. 'That's enough, I think. We don't want to catch pneumonia.'

'No,' Midge agreed, closing the door reluctantly. 'We have problems enough.'

They paused in the doorway of the drawing-room and looked around. Bramwell Barbour now appeared to be in a state of advanced distress, still pinioned firmly by his mother to Lauren-Brigid's side.

'Mmm,' Ned said. 'Looks as though we ought to mount a rescue mission, wouldn't you say?'

'I suppose so,' Midge agreed unwillingly. Lauren or Brigid, whichever she might be, seemed calm and complacent at the moment, happy in her own little dream world with Bramwell Barbour dancing attendance—however reluctant—on her. It might disturb her precarious balance if strangers intruded on them.

Before they could move, Algie broke away from Petronella and her questioners and advanced on the Barbour group with a determined look on his face.

'Oh, good,' Midge said. 'Algie's going over. We won't need to.'

'All the more reason.' Ned moved forward, his own face grimly determined. 'I hate to sound bitchy, but I'm afraid it was type-casting when they sent Old Algie down here to play the bounder. He's fastening on that poor girl like a leech.'

Admiring Ned's selfless disinterest, Midge followed him out of sheer curiosity. Bramwell greeted their approach with relief. Amaryllis glared at them.

'There now, Brigid, here comes *your* beau,' Lauren said, with a flirtatious toss of her head towards Ned.

'Why not?' she promptly answered herself. 'You've got *your's* here—' Another flirtatious toss of the head, this time towards Algie.

'Girls, girls—' Amaryllis said indulgently. 'Don't tease poor Bramwell. You'll break his heart.'

They—she—giggled, bridling.

For the first time, Midge saw Bramwell give his mother a look of intense dislike—almost hatred.

'About time he had some competition, isn't it, Brigid?'

'Sure is, Lauren. He's had things his own way far too long.'

'Girls, you're being very naughty.' Amaryllis regarded the giggling woman complacently. The thought that she might acquire two daughters-in-law rolled into one obviously didn't disturb her a bit. There would also be two fortunes rolled into one. 'Tell poor Bramwell you didn't mean it.'

'Maybe we *did* mean it!' Another toss of the head. 'Maybe we're getting tired of the way Bramwell takes us for granted.'

Bramwell clearly did not wish to take them—or her—at all. He had lost colour and begun backing away. Algie leaped forward to take his place by her side. She smiled coyly at Algie as he took her hand and raised it to his lips.

'Oh, you Englishmen—' She darted a sly sideways glance at Bramwell. 'You're so sophisticated.'

Ned had been moving in to take up a position on her other side, now he halted suddenly. Midge followed his gaze and discovered that Algie had unwittingly claimed the attention of a large segment of the audience.

'Look at that,' Alice Dain said indignantly. 'The minute poor Petronella is in trouble, he runs off and leaves her and goes chasing another woman.'

'That's men for you every time,' Bertha Stout snorted.

'Are you going to let him get away with that?' Alice demanded of Petronella. 'He's *your* boyfriend.'

'He *was*,' someone snickered.

Unnoticed, except perhaps by Amaryllis, Bramwell slipped still farther into the background and disappeared in the direction of the lobby.

Petronella had gone an unattractive shade of red, almost as though she were actually in the process of being jilted. All eyes were on her, waiting for her reaction to Alice's challenge.

'Algie—' Her voice rose in an uneven pitch. 'Algie!'

Algie was bending closer to Lauren-Brigid, patting the

hand that could write large cheques, alert to her slightest word. Petronella's call went unheeded.

Ned might be right about him, Midge decided. Although he was neglecting the script, he was still in character. The fortune-hunting cad was simply on the trail of a larger fortune.

'Don't trouble your pretty little head about that rat, Cousin Pet.' Ned, either more aware of the exigencies of the situation, or bowing to the realization that he had momentarily lost place to Algie with the Chandler twin, crossed to Petronella's side. 'You're well rid of him. Isn't she—?' he appealed to the audience.

'She sure is!'

'Forget him, honey, that kind's no good to anybody.'

'Come back to the States with us and take your rightful place as head of Van Dine Industries.'

'Don't let it get you down—there's plenty more fish in the sea.'

Advice showered on the Hon. Pet from all sides. She appeared oblivious of them all, her attention focused on the defecting Algie. And Lauren-Brigid.

'Boy! If looks could kill! I wouldn't take any bets on the other one being around much longer.'

'That's a rotten thing to say!' Reminded of unpleasant reality, public opinion swung to censure the offending speaker. 'You're not suggesting Petronella could have had anything to do with *that*?'

'Why not? Somebody did. You've been suspecting her of killing Sir Cedric, Lady Hermione and Miss Holloway, so why not Brigid Chandler, too?'

'Because—because—' Because that was real and the others were make-believe, but the complaint stuck in Alice's craw. Everyone knew what she meant.

'Shh!' After a quick guilty glance towards Lauren. 'She's listening.'

'Ladies and gentlemen—' Reggie had returned and was making an announcement from the bar. 'We're sorry that your holiday has been disrupted by this shocking series of events. Until the highways are cleared and the police get through to us, we'll try to do our best to make it up to you. As a start, all drinks are on the house for the rest of the evening.'

The distraction worked. Despite the jeers and catcalls, there was a rush to the bar.

'Do you think we ought to? Those drinks aren't safe.'

'I just hope we aren't heading for *Death At The Bar*.'

'Talk about living dangerously!'

Midge went beyond the bar, pulled back the drape concealing the French window, and gazed out over the terrace, heaped with drifted snow. The stone urns on the corners of the stone railing overflowed with glittering crystals. Momentarily forgetting everything but the beauty of the scene, Midge began to plan an expedition with her camera in the morning. A shot of the snow-encrusted terrace from the garden below ought to make a perfect Christmas card to send to guests who had stayed at the Manor throughout the year.

Then she remembered what morning was likely to bring in reality. She closed her eyes against the knowledge.

'Where every prospect pleases—' Dix had come up behind her—'And only man is vile . . .'

'Yes.' Midge let the drape fall back into place and turned away. 'I was just thinking something of the sort myself.'

CHAPTER 18

The guests lingered late over their drinks. And lingered . . . and lingered . . .

Having once made his escape, Bramwell never returned. Shortly thereafter, Evelina had slipped away. Later still, the actors had retired, with the exception of Algie, who was still paying court to Lauren-Brigid.

'Midge, do you think we ought to do something?' Having served yet another brace of drinks to the lady, plus one for the gentleman, Reggie had returned to her considerably shaken.

'What can we do?'

'I don't know, but it's getting serious. I couldn't help overhearing Algie murmuring those famous three little words to her. Followed by a couple of more sinister ones: "Special Licence". He can't do that, can he? I mean, the woman's crackers.'

'Not half as crackers as Algie is,' Midge said. 'How does he think he could put up with that day after day?'

'I shouldn't think he's planning on a long-term venture,' Reggie said. 'She's from California; don't they have a Community Property Law there? He'll stay with her for a couple of years, then get a divorce and walk off with half her money.'

'Leaving her financially just where she was before her sister died.'

'You don't think she killed her own twin?' Reggie was shocked, but ready to believe anything. 'Just for money?'

'And for exclusive rights to Bramwell,' Midge said. 'Don't forget that.'

'I thought they'd parcelled him out between them quite amicably.' Reggie shuddered. 'I wouldn't blame him if he'd been the one to murder her. In self-defence.'

'Much good that would do him while the other one was still alive. His mother is going to serve him up on toast to whichever one wants him.'

'Aha! You noticed that, did you?' Dix was there behind her.

'Oh!' Midge jumped. 'You startled me.'

'My apologies. I didn't mean to. I thought you'd seen me.'

'No, I was watching Amaryllis.'

'Ah yes.' He followed her gaze. 'On her way to break up the little *tête-à-tête*. How touching. Looking after her son's interests—whether he wants her to or not. A woman who bears watching, indeed.'

Curled up in her armchair, obviously exhausted but unwilling to leave while so many of her tour were still awake and alert, Roberta Rinehart watched also.

The lights were low, the gramophone had been allowed to wind down, conversation was muted and relaxed. Outside, the wind had risen and the occasional patter of snowflakes against the window-panes was caused by the wind redistributing the drifted snow. When Midge had checked a short while ago, it had seemed a softer, milder wind, holding promise of spring and plant life stirring in the chill earth beneath the blanket of snow.

'Oh!'

'What the—!'

Amaryllis had abruptly switched the floor lamp behind the armchair to full power. Algie had been sitting on the arm of the chair, murmuring to Lauren. They both blinked in the glare of harsh light, the mood of intimacy broken.

'It's late,' Amaryllis cooed. 'And dear Lauren should take a sleeping pill and go to bed. She's had a very fraught day.'

'What about Brigid?' Lauren protested. 'I'm not going to go to bed and leave her staying up having all the fun!'

'Brigid, too,' Amaryllis said smoothly, although those around winced. 'Come along, girls—Both of you—' Amaryllis took her by both hands and tugged her gently out of the chair.

'She shouldn't take any sleeping pills,' Midge worried. 'She's had too much to drink.'

'She'll probably go to sleep as soon as her head hits the pillow.' Reggie had gained a professional barman's ability to judge capacities over the past couple of tours. 'Amaryllis will be lucky if she gets her that far before she passes out.'

'Can Algie come too?' Leaning heavily against Amaryllis, Lauren allowed herself to be half-carried towards the door. Algie stepped forward, as though to help, but Amaryllis gave him such a vicious glare that he stepped back.

'Algie wants another drink first,' Amaryllis lied soothingly. 'But I'll tell you what. I'm sure Bramwell will want to come in and say good night to you before you fall asleep. You'd like that, wouldn't you?'

'I don't know—' Lauren shrugged, throwing them both off-course. 'Algie's kinda sweet and he's got the cutest English accent. Maybe I'll keep him for myself and let Brigid have Bramwell.'

'Oh, now, you don't want to be too hasty—' Amaryllis had gone pale. Her burden was rapidly becoming almost a dead weight, she staggered slightly.

'Let me help you.' Reggie went over to them as they hesitated at the foot of the staircase.

'I should think you would! I don't know why you don't have an elevator in this place.' Amaryllis dared not criticize her daughter-in-law-elect, so she expended her fury on Reggie. 'It's ridiculous to set yourself up as a hotel and not have the commonest amenities. I've a good mind to complain to the English Tourist Board about you!'

Reggie's lips tightened, but he took his place at Lauren's other side and let most of her weight shift over to him. Amaryllis's voice faded, still complaining, as they mounted the stairs.

Algie snapped off the lamp spotlighting the now empty chair and stood irresolutely for a moment before turning and leaving the room. Someone sighed faintly, as though being released from a spell.

'*Whee-ew* . . .' The atmosphere lightened immediately. 'Thank heavens they're gone.'

'That's a rotten thing to say after all that poor girl has gone through.'

'Believe me, I have every sympathy—but you can't deny she's sure a skeleton at the feast.'

'I figure it this way,' Stan said seriously. 'It could have been worse. It could have been someone we liked.'

There was an uneasy rustle of agreement. Perhaps, Midge thought, it was because the Chandler twins were so disliked that the situation had remained under control. They were no loss to anyone. Their absence was marked by relief rather than mourning. Bramwell might even find it a cause for celebration. Especially if the other twin were also to be removed. So long as one of them was still alive, his mother would give him no peace. Especially now that Algie had tossed his hat into the ring.

'Speaking of a feast—' Dix changed the subject. 'I would like to propose a Vote of Thanks to our hostess—our proper hostess—' he bowed to Midge—'for the splendid feast she has placed before us. Food for the mind and spirit, as well as the body. Never did I hope to participate in such a splendid re-creation of a Golden Age house-party, complete with the Murder Game you English invented—'

'They did not!' The single dissenting voice of Bertha Stout rose above the murmur of agreement.

'I beg your pardon?' Dix frowned at her.

'They didn't invent the Murder Game.' Bertha stood her ground. 'It was introduced into England by Elsa Maxwell at the party to open Lady Ribblesdale's house in St James's Park in the 1920s. And Maxwell herself admitted that she didn't originate the game. It was invented by another American woman, the artist, Neysa McMein—'

'One of the Algonquin Round Table,' Dix said quickly.

'Right. It caused a sensation because Maxwell rigged it so that the guilty party appeared to be the Duke of Marlborough. He was stunned, but took it in good part. But the Press heard about it and the *Daily Express* carried the story on the front page. The public thought it sounded like a great idea and the Murder Game swept the country. So much so that it was believed to be an English invention. Especially after it was immortalized in Ngaio Marsh's first book—'

'*A Man Lay Dead*—1934.' Dix was still trying to regain control of the conversation.

'Of course, with the war and its aftermath, such frivolity disappeared for a long time—'

'I wouldn't say that.' Dix tried again. 'Agatha Christie used it as late as 1956 in *Dead Man's Folly*.'

'These murder weekends—' Bertha overrode him firmly —'are in direct descent from the Murder Game of the Golden Age. And I agree with Dix, Midge, you've done a splendid job. It's just too bad some spoilsport has stepped in to settle a personal score and ruined all your efforts.'

'Thank you,' Midge said faintly. 'I'm just sorry that your holiday has ended like this.'

'It hasn't ended yet.' Bertha rose and lurched towards the bar, having noticed that Reggie had returned to his duties there.

'Last orders,' Reggie announced, giving notice that the evening was over so far as he was concerned and the bar was closing. 'Last orders, please.'

'Gee—' Alice tittered nervously. 'I sure hope they won't be.'

Morning dawned bright and mild. The weather forecast was for a warmer spell now that the weekend was nearly over and people had to return to work. The news featured reports of arctic conditions still gripping the country. Their area, they discovered, was far from being the worst off. Food was being dropped by helicopter to remote villages in Scotland and Wales. Farmers were struggling to dig out flocks of sheep buried beneath the snow. Emergency crews were working overtime to clear highways and it was hoped that another twenty-four hours would see most of the country back to normal.

Operating on the principle that everyone liked to sleep late on a Sunday morning, breakfast was served buffet-style from covered silver-plated serving dishes set out on side-boards in the dining-room. By nine o'clock several of the guests were prowling along the sideboards, tilting back the domed covers to reveal scrambled eggs, bacon, sausages, kedgeree, devilled kidneys, kippers and hot toast. (The first barrage of complaints had taught them that Americans took their toast seriously and were not willing to eat it cold from toast racks, as the English did.)

Lettie rushed round with pots of steaming tea or coffee as soon as they had seated themselves.

Once they had settled with their food, those so favoured brought out the new clues, in the form of the anonymous letters they had had slipped under their doors in the early hours of the morning.

'*Did Grace Holloway leave a Will?*' Bertha read out with relish. '*There is no next of kin. She had lived at the Manor for ten years—so who inherits from her?*'

Bertha and the people at her table turned as one to stare at Lettie as she brought round tea and coffee. Midge paused in the doorway, watching with amusement as Lettie went about her chores unsuspectingly. There had been no time to warn her about the extra clue, hastily composed to cover the murder of Miss Holloway.

'*Ask Eric—*' Haila Bond read out to her table— '*why he suddenly ended his self-imposed exile in Ceylon. Did he come back to help his daughter—or to escape from another scandal?*'

Midge backed away quickly as Haila's table began to buzz with speculation and look around eagerly. Except for Lettie, none of the actors had come down for breakfast yet. This was according to the revised schedule to draw out the proceedings. Had they not been snowbound, the solution of the case would have been served up with coffee at elevenses. As it was, the solution was now planned for late afternoon, then the post-mortems could occupy them at dinner, followed by a relaxing evening when everyone could unwind.

Everyone except the real murderer. Reggie was going to try to get through to town during the night and, unbeknownst to the guests, bring the police back in the morning to carry out the genuine murder inquiry. Meanwhile, the longer the air of unreality continued, the better. If the killer could be lulled into a false sense of security, it might prevent him from trying to dispatch the remaining Chandler twin. If he thought he had plenty of time, he might delay striking.

Meanwhile, they must keep a close watch over her.

Eric was hiding out in the kitchen. He slumped at the table, staring moodily at the printing on the muesli box.

'No *Sunday Times*,' he complained bitterly. 'No newspapers at all. One of the things I was looking forward to about being home was being able to read the newspapers the same day they were printed. Now here I am—and not one bloody newspaper delivered!'

'You were lucky you were able to get yourself through the blizzard,' Midge said unsympathetically. 'You can't expect a poor little newsboy to struggle through those drifts.'

Ackroyd came forward at hearing her voice and registered a bitter complaint of his own. Midge looked down and saw that Eric had half-filled a saucer with muesli and not added enough milk even to wet it through. It was no way to treat a hungry cat. No wonder Ackroyd was complaining.

'All right, Ackroyd, I don't blame you.' She crossed to get a tin of cat food from the store cupboard. 'Come on, treats!' She reached for the tin-opener.

Ackroyd hurried after her, chirruping happily. This was more like it. He wound round her ankles as she opened the tin and filled his dish.

Midge bent to place the dish on the floor. Ackroyd rose on his hind legs to meet it.

'Just one moment!' The dish was suddenly snatched away from both of them.

'What—?' Midge straightened to meet Dixon Carr's triumphant eyes. Ackroyd yowled indignantly. 'What on earth do you think you're doing, Mr Carr?'

'Oh no, Midge. The question is: what are *you* doing?'

'Feeding Ackroyd. Anyone can see that.'

'Aha! That's what they're meant to see.' He nodded as though he had scored a point. 'But—are you feeding him? Or poisoning him?'

'Oh, not again! Are you mad? Why should I want to poison Ackroyd?'

'You deny it, then?'

'I most certainly do! And I'll thank you to give Ackroyd his breakfast. He's hungry.'

'You swear that this dish is innocent of poison?'

'I most certainly do.'

'In that case—' he held it out to her—'you won't object to tasting it yourself.'

'Don't be absurd, Mr Carr,' Midge said coldly. 'That's cat food. Tinned cat food.'

'Precisely!' he said. 'And this is a hotel. With an excellent dining-room serving three meals a day. There must be enough scraps to feed several cats. So why are you giving him tinned cat food?'

'Because he happens to like it. Liver is a great favourite of his and we don't serve it often because so many people dislike it. I opened that tin to give Ackroyd a special treat. Will you be good enough to let him have it?'

'Oh—' Dix looked from her angry eyes, to the dish in his hand, to the furious, impatient cat.

'This has gone far enough!' Midge took the dish from him and placed it on the floor. Ackroyd immediately hunched over it, growling menacingly as he began to gulp it down.

'I—I'm afraid I've upset you.'

'*That* is an understatement. Furthermore, you shouldn't be here at all. The kitchen is out of bounds.'

'I know. I'm sorry. It's just that I got so worried when I found that warning shoved under my door—'

'What warning?'

'This warning.' He pulled a piece of paper from his pocket, unfolded it and passed it to her.

'BEWARE—' was printed in block capital letters— 'NOT ALL CATS HAVE NINE LIVES.'

'You see,' he said earnestly, reclaiming the note and frowning at it. 'You can see why I got so worried. I thought of Ackroyd immediately. Maybe there was some way he could give the murderer away. Maybe somebody was out to get him.'

'I see.' Midge tried not to sound puzzled. 'Although I think your concern is misplaced. Ackroyd is no threat to anyone.'

'I hope you're right.'

'In any case, I must ask you to leave Ackroyd's safety to me. In fact—'

'In fact, you'd like me to leave. All right. I apologize for disturbing you.' He turned and left the kitchen.

'Eric,' Midge said thoughtfully. 'Eric, I thought all the anonymous letters were going to be pasted-up newsprint. I didn't know you'd hand-lettered any of them.'

'We didn't,' Eric said promptly. 'If it wasn't pasted-up, it wasn't one of ours. He should have got one suggesting Lettie was Miss Holloway's illegitimate daughter.'

'But he didn't,' Midge said. 'He got one saying all cats didn't have nine lives.'

'Then that anonymous letter is an impostor. Somebody else is playing their own game. Is it something to do with curiosity killing the cat, do you suppose?'

'I don't know,' Midge said slowly, 'but I don't like it. Just in case, I'm keeping Ackroyd behind the scenes until all those people have left.'

CHAPTER 19

The actors stood up well to the brisk round of renewed questioning, but Eric was completely out of his depth. Although game, he had picked up a few Australian expressions which were leading even the most trusting questioners to suspect that he had not spent his entire exile in Ceylon. This was all to the good, of course, as it opened new fields of speculation.

In a burst of inspiration, Evelina invited everyone to a pre-luncheon sherry party in her rooms. Not to be outdone, Amaryllis promptly announced that Bramwell would be serving more realistic drinks in his quarters.

The parties started early and overflowed into the corridor. Traffic was brisk from one party to the other, some people lodged permanently in the hallway, moving only to fetch a fresh drink. A general air of hilarity began to prevail.

Unfortunately, this meant that the rooms weren't getting done. Since Hermione and Grace were officially dead, they could not make an appearance until they had taken their bows at the solution. Lettie had been co-opted by Evelina to help serve the sherry. Across the hallway, Amaryllis had pressed Lauren-Brigid into service. Perhaps that was another reason Evelina's party was more popular than Bramwell's.

Even Bramwell seemed to prefer it to his own. Amaryllis had to cross over periodically to retrieve him.

'Bramwell, you're neglecting your guests. And—' with a sly glance towards Lettie—'your poor little fiancée.'

'She's *not* my fiancée.' Bramwell, too, glanced towards Lettie and raised his voice. 'I never asked her to marry me. I don't even like her.'

'Bramwell!' His mother used a tone of shocked reproof. 'After all those poor girls have been through—'

'I didn't like them at the best of times,' Bramwell said stubbornly. 'Now one of them is dead and the other one is certifiable. I should think—' he gambled recklessly—'you'd want your grandchildren to have a better background than that.'

'You can leave that to me,' Amaryllis said crisply. 'When I look at you—and remember your father—I'm convinced of the triumph of environment over heredity!'

The luncheon gong sounded from the dining-room below. Was it a coincidence that Lettie had disappeared?

The Honourable Petronella led the way down the staircase, Algie on one side of her, Edwin Lupin on the other. She favoured them with equal smiles, equal dollops of conversation. It was remarked, however, that once in the dining-room she abandoned them both and went to sit between Eric and Colonel Heather.

Algie promptly looked round for Lauren-Brigid, found her, and rushed to elbow aside an unresisting Bramwell in order to claim the seat next to her.

Amaryllis, already seated on the other side, glowered with impotent fury at her son as he cheerfully left the field to his rival and moved to a vacant seat at Evelina's table.

There were worse problems to worry about, however.

'Look—' Roberta Rinehart drew Midge aside. 'I'm scared. I mean, when you start unrolling the solution later on and the "victims" come out to take their bows—what's it going to do to Lauren? It will hit her all over again about her twin. I wouldn't like to be responsible for what might happen.'

'Neither would I,' Midge said. 'But there's another reason we'll have to keep an eye on Lauren. Dix got a real anonymous letter—one we didn't write ourselves. It said not all cats have nine lives. It may mean that Brigid was killed in mistake for Lauren—both twins were catty enough. It might just be that someone is playing games with us. Or it might be a genuine threat.'

'Oh God!' Roberta bit her lip. 'It ould even be the murderer playing games with us—in the best tradition. That's the trouble, they're all steeped in the Golden Age. Any one of them might have done it. I wish we'd never started these tours!'

Midge had been wishing that herself earlier. Now, hearing Roberta say it, she felt a strange pang. It had been such fun —up until this group. She hadn't realized how much she had been hoping they'd go on with it. If Roberta were to pull out—

'We'll ask Amaryllis to look after Lauren,' Midge said. 'She can get her out of the way and keep her out of the way while Reggie delivers the solution.'

'Yes, but—'

But that didn't solve the problem of what to do with her

for the rest of the night—and tomorrow. Cedric, Hermione and Grace could hardly be expected to hide themselves away until the tour left. It was difficult enough as it was.

'We'll worry about that later,' Midge said. 'I've got to help with the serving now.' She sidestepped Roberta and retreated to the kitchen.

Cook was in a state of nerves, rehearsing her impending big scene. Her apron was streaked with lipstick marks and, as Midge watched, she tossed it towards her head again. It swung upwards, flapped over the top of her head, then slid downwards. There was a fresh crimson streak on it as it fell into place over her ample stomach.

'It's no use,' Cook wailed. 'I'll never be able to make that thing stay over my face. Can't we let someone else do it?'

'Sorry, love,' Lettie said. 'You're the only one they haven't seen. The surprise witness—it's got to be you. Perhaps,' she added critically, 'we could sew a coin in the corners to weight it, the way they do with drapes.'

'Suppose I hit myself with it and get a black eye?'

'A black eye won't show up until later—' Lettie was not conscious of heartlessness, she was too involved in the mechanics of the problem. 'It wouldn't matter.'

'Not to *you*—'

'How about your lines?' Lettie interrupted briskly. 'Have you got them pat?'

'I think so. When Master Reggie calls me in—'

'Reggie, Reggie,' Reggie said. 'Better still, just Reg. I'm supposed to be one of the hired help, too. You'll give the game away—'

'I can't remember everything,' Cook wailed.

'You're doing fine,' Lettie said swiftly. 'Just keep calm. We'll get you a fresh apron, stitch a tenpenny piece in each corner, then all you'll have to do is—'

'How about serving lunch first?' Midge reminded them. 'The guests are all out there waiting.'

'Coffee will be served in the lounge,' Midge announced at the end of lunch. To reach the lounge, unlike the drawing-room, they would have to pass through the lobby. She wondered who would be the first to spot the new addition to the notice board.

No one even looked. Most of them drifted through the lobby still carrying on the conversations they had started at their tables. A few were silent and preoccupied—to the point of moroseness. Nearly everyone looked to the windows to check on whether the snow had started again. The lowering grey sky obviously filled them with apprehension.

Midge held a hurried consultation with Roberta and Reggie; they agreed that it would be well to speed up events again—before people had too much time to brood. Roberta then went off to have a quiet word with Amaryllis.

Midge then went into the lounge and made an announcement.

'My husband, who, as you know, is an ex-Scotland Yard man, thinks he now knows who murdered Sir Cedric, Lady Hermione and Miss Holloway—and why. However, he would be glad to have any help you can give him to verify his conclusions so that he can make an arrest.'

'Can he make an arrest if he isn't with Scotland Yard any longer?' a sceptic wanted to know.

'We all have the power to make a Citizen's Arrest,' Midge said with dignity.

'She's right.'

'No, she's not.'

'Could we? We're not citizens of this country.'

'Please—' Midge clapped her hands, calling them back to order. 'Reggie will join us soon. Meanwhile, you'll find a stack of Deduction Sheets on the table beneath the notice board. If you would kindly answer the questions, stating your candidate for the killer—and the motives—and give them to me, I'll take them to Reggie so that he can study them and see if any of you have found any clues he may have overlooked.'

There was a concerted rush for the lobby to collect Deduction Sheets. Once everyone was milling around out there, it did not take them long to discover the fresh clue.

'Hey—look! Where did that come from?'

'What is it?'

'A ring. A gold wedding ring on a thin gold chain. And see, the chain's broken. It must have fallen off someone.'

'Who? And who found it? Who put it up there?'

'Where did they find it?'

'Take it down. Let's have a closer look.' Bertha Stout reached up and detached the chain and ring from the drawing-pin.

'Careful—fingerprints,' someone warned.

'Nonsense!' Colonel Heather snorted. 'Little thing like that wouldn't take any prints. And how could you bring them out?'

'You seem to know a lot about it.' They looked at him with renewed suspicion.

'You don't happen to recognize the ring, do you, Colonel . . . *Heather*?' Dix asked meaningly.

'Never saw it before in my life.'

'There are initials inside!' Bertha had been examining the ring, now she held it up and squinted into it. 'Can't quite make them out—'

'Let me see!' Haila Bond snatched at the ring. Bertha tried to hold on, but was left with the thin chain dangling from her fingers, while Haila held the ring, twisting it so that light fell on the initials.

'It looks like . . . AC and CS . . .' she reported. 'And there's a date . . . 1914.'

'Are you sure?'

'Who are they?'

'CS—Cedric Strangeways!' Bertha had it. 'But who's AC?'

'Sir Cedric was married? Then what was he doing getting a marriage licence with Lettie?'

'Did Lettie find out? Did she kill him in a fury?'

'Maybe AC found out about Lettie.'

'I know Sir Cedric was absent-minded—but could he really forget he had a wife?'

'Maybe he thought he could get away with bigamy.'

'How do we know AC is still alive?'

'Maybe she isn't any longer. Maybe Grace Holloway wasn't her real name and—'

They were well away. Midge relaxed again. More so, when she heard Amaryllis speak softly to Lauren, as instructed:

'There's about an inch or so missing from that chain. Why don't we go and look for it? We'll solve the case ourselves and surprise everyone.'

'Yes, let's.' Enthusiastically, Lauren followed Amaryllis up the staircase, not realizing that she was to be kept safely out of the way for the next hour.

'All right.' Midge nodded to Lettie, who stood poised near the kitchen door. 'Wheel Cook on.'

Lettie nodded back and disappeared.

'A piece of this chain is missing.' Bertha came to the same conclusion as Amaryllis, but unaided. 'About an inch and a half, including part of the clasp.' She looked around suspiciously. 'Maybe we'll find it clutched in the hand of the next corpse.'

'Oh, Bertha—that's awful!' Alice Dain shuddered.

'Good thinking,' Asey said. 'Is anybody missing?'

'Practically everybody.' Bertha found gloomy satisfaction in this. 'Don't you see? They've disappeared because it's time for us to decide whodunit.'

'But, if you think there's another body to be found—'

'It might not be another murder—it might be a suicide. The easy way out. Remember, this is 1935—and the death penalty is still in force. They swing for murder!'

'Oh, Bertha—that's even more awful! I don't—' Alice broke off as the rattle of china caught her attention. She turned. 'Why—who's that?'

They all turned as Cook moved past them, head down, wheeling the trolley into the lounge.

'Yeah—' Asey started after her. 'Where did she come from? We haven't seen her before. Hey—you! You—wait a minute—' He grabbed Cook's arm, bringing her to a reluctant halt. 'Who are you?'

'I—? I'm Cook, sir. Lettie is terribly busy, so I've brought in the coffee things for her.'

'What do you mean—Cook?' Bertha advanced on her, quivering with suspicion. 'Do you mean you are the cook, or do you mean your name is Cook?'

'B—both.' Cook stood her ground with some difficulty, she had not been prepared to meet such intensity. 'Cook by name and Cook by nature, I always say.'

'And I suppose you've always worked at the Manor?'

'Oh yes, ma'am. Ever since I was a child and started out as the 'tweenie.''

'C for Cook,' Bertha said reflectively. 'I think we're getting there. And what's your first name?'

'Everyone always calls me Cook.'

'I've no doubt they do, but you must have a first name. What is it?'

'It's—' Cook looked to Midge, who nodded encouragingly. 'It's Agatha.'

'Agatha!'

'And what's wrong with that?' Cook flared. 'It's a perfectly good name.'

'An excellent name,' Bertha said triumphantly. 'And it makes you AC—who married Sir Cedric Strangeways in 1914!'

'How did you—?' Cook clutched at her neck, her fingers searching for something they failed to find.

'Is this what you're looking for?' Haila held the gold ring up before her.

'Where did you get that?' Cook grabbed for it, but Haila was faster. 'Give me that—it's mine!'

'Just as I thought!' Bertha said. 'The Son of the House and the—what were you by then? The housemaid? Parlour maid? Apprentice cook? Anyway, it was a secret wartime marriage—and there was only one reason for that in those days. You were carrying his child, weren't you?'

'No—' Cook said. 'No—'

'Yes,' Bertha insisted. 'You were a young girl, he had got you in trouble—and he was an honourable man. He was also on his way to the Front. He knew he might never come back. He gave you the protection of his name. He legitimized his child.'

'No,' Cook cried. 'No—it wasn't his!' She got the apron over her head at the first throw and stumbled back to the kitchen before anyone could stop her.

'I'm sorry—' Midge moved forward to intercept as they tried to chase after Cook. 'That's enough for now. Cook is too upset. She never thought her guilty secret would be revealed. You must give her time to recover herself—or we won't have any dinner tonight.'

Grumbling, they let themselves be shepherded into the lounge. They were annotating their papers frantically, deep in a new wave of speculation.

'Whatever else, we sure can't accuse Sir Cedric of being a snob. First he married his cook, then he tried to marry his parlourmaid.'

'Maybe Cook killed him—because she was jealous.'

'Were they divorced? We never got a chance to ask.'

'Maybe Lettie was Cook's daughter and Cook killed him to stop him from committing incest.'

'Naw—she said the kid wasn't his.'

'Did he know it, I wonder?'

'If he didn't, all the more reason. He wouldn't try to marry Lettie if he thought she was his daughter.'

'Anyway, *my* anonymous letter as good as said Lettie was Miss Holloway's illegitimate daughter. So there'd be no problem in that case.'

'There's an awful lot of illegitimacy around here,' Alice complained.

'Yeah,' Stan agreed. 'Who was fathering all these little bastards?'

'I'll ask you to let me have your Deduction Sheets in five minutes,' Midge warned. 'Reggie is waiting.'

'Listen, everyone.' Roberta clapped her hands for attention. 'We mustn't forget that the time has also come for you to choose between the Honourable Petronella and Edward Lupin. Which one is to take their place at the head of Van Dine Industries?'

'Oh no—not another problem! How are we going to choose?'

'A secret ballot is the only way,' Roberta said. 'Bramwell will give out and then collect the voting slips. If you'll write down the name of your choice, I will then count the votes and announce your decision.'

'One damn thing after another,' Stan grumbled. 'How are we supposed to vote when one of them might be the murderer?'

'You're supposed to have figured that out first,' Bertha said. 'Haven't you? I have.'

'So have I,' Haila said.

'Oh, it's so difficult,' Alice complained.

'You have all the clues,' Roberta said.

'I'd hate to bet on that,' Asey hooted.

'You have all the clues,' Roberta repeated firmly. 'Now, sit down and vote.'

CHAPTER 20

Midge collected the Deduction Sheets and brought them out to Reggie, then Bramwell gave out the ballot slips. While they were absorbed in their voting, Lettie quietly returned and began serving coffee.

Unobtrusively, the other actors filed into the lounge and seated themselves among the guests. Evelina T. Carterslee nodded congratulations to Midge; all was going well.

Reggie, having donned a business suit and carrying a

clipboard crammed with Deduction Sheets and other papers, made his entrance, looking sombre and official. He seated himself beside Roberta at the table that had been set up at one end of the lounge.

Bramwell delivered the ballot slips to Roberta. Midge brought coffee to both of them and retreated to stand against the wall where she could best observe the scene. The expectant hush as Roberta and Reggie studied their respective piles of paper was broken by excited whispers and the clatter of cups from the audience.

At last, Reggie pushed his clipboard aside and nodded to Roberta. She looked down at the two piles of slips in front of her; one was noticeably higher than the other.

'The decision about the fate of Van Dine Industries was very close.' Tactfully, she ignored the evidence of the slips before her.

'However, the vote seems to have gone in favour of one —on a conditional basis. The consensus of opinion is that the new head of Van Dine Industries should be the Honourable Petronella Van Dine—but only if she renounces Algernon Moriarty.'

'Oh, I say,' Algie complained. 'That's a bit thick. You're not going to do it, are you, Pet?'

Petronella rose to her feet. There was a long, thoughtful silence.

'I—I feel I have a duty to—to my heritage,' she faltered. 'I'm sorry, Algie—'

'It's *my* heritage, too!' Ned leaped to his feet, quivering with fury. 'I'll fight this decision to the highest court in the land.'

'Boy, what a sore loser!' someone commented. 'He'd have been a lousy boss.'

'Oh, well—' Algie rose and began strolling casually towards the door. 'In that case, I might as well toddle along. There's nothing here for me—'

'Don't let him get away!' Reggie snapped.

Norman Dain and Stanley Marric caught Algie as he

began to run for the exit. They brought him, struggling wildly, to stand before Reggie.

'Algernon Moriarty,' Reggie said solemnly, 'I hereby arrest you for the murders of Sir Cedric Strangeways, Lady Hermione Marsh and Miss Grace Holloway.'

'It's a lie!' Algie shouted. 'Why should I kill them?'

'In order to inherit Chortlesby Manor,' Reggie said.

'Aha—I guessed it!' Dix said.

'No! No! It's a lie! I didn't do it! Tell them—' He appealed to the motionless form hovering in the doorway. 'Tell them I didn't do it, Mummy.'

'I was afraid of this—' Cook delivered her last line. 'There was always bad blood in that boy!' She flipped the apron over her head and disappeared again.

'Bad blood,' Reggie said solemnly. 'But Strangeways blood. There was only one reason Sir Cedric would have sacrificed himself by marrying Cook—to give his father's child the family name! He never expected to return from the Front and so he thought it didn't matter.'

'But Algie's name is Moriarty,' Alice said in bewilderment.

'Quite so.' Reggie spoke rapidly, gradually speeding up even more, to race through the explanation at breakneck pace. 'Once Sir Cedric—or Cedric, as he was then—returned safely, although wounded, from the Front, the succession was no longer in doubt. He—and he alone—would inherit Chortlesby Manor. A different future had to be arranged for his half-brother. It was—is—traditional to buy younger sons a commission in the Army, and this was done as soon as Algie, graduating from a minor Public School, was old enough. For reasons best known to himself, Algie changed his name at that time. He then proceeded to bring disgrace upon his new name.'

'Curse you, Dain!' Algie struggled anew with his captors. 'Let me go!'

'His family lost track of him under his new name—perhaps they never knew it. No one had seen him since he was sent away to school as a child, he had changed a great deal as he grew up. When he encountered Lady Hermione —with the Honourable Petronella under her wing—in London, he recognized her, although she did not recognize him, and saw his chance. A double chance. Petronella was his key to Chortlesby Manor. And, if he could persuade her to marry him as well, he would have an heiress bride whose fortune could maintain him in the Manor to which he wished to become accustomed.'

Undeterred by groans, Reggie continued his summation.

'By this time, Cook, his mother, had learned of Sir Cedric's plan to marry Lettie. If the marriage had taken place and there had subsequently been children of that marriage, Algie's chances of succeeding would have been dashed. His only hope was to kill his half-brother before the marriage could take place. It had only been delayed in order to allow Lady Hermione time to reconcile herself to the match. But Algie also knew that, if he put forward his claim after Sir Cedric's death, his half-sister would know immediately that he had been responsible. So he had to kill her, too.'

'And Miss Holloway knew too much,' several people chorused. She had established that beautifully.

'That is correct. Miss Holloway was the sort of person everyone trusts and confides in. She met Sir Cedric when she worked in the office of the solicitor who handled his eventual divorce. They became friends and he invited her to take up residence at the Manor when she had no other place to go when she retired.'

'Beautiful!' Dix said. 'Beautiful!'

'Take him away!' Reggie ordered Algie's captors. They marched Algie out of the lounge.

'So there we are,' Roberta said. 'The solution to *Murder At The Manor*.' She led the applause.

One by one, the actors stood up and took their bows. Algie came back into the lounge, Norman and Stanley behind him. They seemed to feel that they were entitled to bows, too.

'Great!' Bertha gave a sigh of satisfaction. 'I was close. I spotted Cook—but I was certain that the child had been a girl. I was even wondering about the Babies Swapped At Birth gimmick. For a while, I suspected that Petronella—'

The happy hubbub of post-mortems filled the lounge. Cedric, Hermione and Grace filed into the room to fresh applause. The audience converged on the actors to congratulate them upon the finer points of their performances.

Lettie slipped away and began collecting the coffee cups and piling them on the trolley. The show might be over, but the ordinary chores of life must go on. 'That went quite well,' she said to Midge.

'Very well.' Midge took possession of the trolley and began wheeling it towards the door.

'Oh-oh!' Lettie said. 'How did she get away?'

Lauren blocked the doorway, surveying the lounge. 'What happened?' she demanded. 'What have I missed?'

'Nothing really, dear—' Forgetting her newly-resurrected state, Miss Holloway came forward to help. 'I can explain everything to you—'

'Someone better,' Lauren said belligerently. 'We're sick and tired of missing everything. You keep doing all the important bits when we're out of the way. It isn't fair!'

'What are you doing down here by yourself?' Midge asked uneasily. 'Where's Amaryllis?'

'Oh, she didn't want us to come down,' Lauren answered carelessly. 'So we locked her in the bathroom.'

'I suppose I ought to go up and let Mother out,' Bramwell said, not very enthusiastically.

'I wouldn't hurry, if I were you,' Cedric advised. 'She's going to be in a foul mood.'

'Yes.' Bramwell shuddered. 'I'm afraid so.'

'Have another drink first,' Dix suggested. They had already had one. 'Fortify yourself.'

'It *is* kind of peaceful without her,' Bertha said.

'Look,' Stan said. 'She isn't going to know how long it took for that loopy dame to tell us where she was. We can act as though we just found out. Another half-hour or so isn't going to make that much difference.'

'She isn't shouting or banging on the door, or any-thing—' Haila returned from a foray into the upper reaches. 'Or, if she is, we can't hear her.'

Amaryllis had brought it on herself, Midge reflected. They had already managed to ignore her plight for over an hour. No one wanted to face the flare of temper when she was finally released. And it *was* lovely and peaceful without her.

It was Midge's last coherent thought for quite a while. They were now well into overtime on this tour. According to the original schedule, the coach should have collected the tour right after lunch and taken them to the airport. While it might be to Roberta's advantage that this had been prevented from happening, it was making a lot more work for everyone at the Manor—especially as they were without outside help.

Eric was in the kitchen chopping onions for Cook, a task he considered more congenial than trying to make conversation with the guests. Lettie, Grace and Hermione had disappeared to make up the rooms while the guests were occupied in the bar with their pre-dinner drinks.

As Midge went back and forth between the kitchen and dining-room setting the tables, she was aware of burst of hilarity from the lounge. Evelina T. Carterslee, an excellent raconteuse when she chose to be, was regaling her fans with some of her favourite stories.

From the bar, Cedric's voice could be heard telling a story of his own about one of the earlier tours: 'Never had so many drinks bought for me in my life. Then I discovered why. Someone had told them I was Charles Paris incognito.'

Everyone seemed to be having a good time. 'The character I'd like to have met,' Stanley Marric said, 'was Arthur

Crook. I could really identify with a rough-diamond kind of lawyer like him.'

That wasn't a bad idea, Midge mused. Perhaps they could do a 'Dinner With the Detectives'. The actors could bone up on a particular sleuth, get his or her cases down pat, so that they could answer questions and keep in character all evening . . . Yes, it was definitely something to bear in mind for future weekends—She broke off, remembering that there might not be any future weekends. And this one wasn't over yet.

'I should think you'd prefer Perry Mason,' Cedric said. 'All those courtroom pyrotechnics—'

'Naw,' Stan said. 'He was too—too American. I'd rather meet these English characters. They've got a lot more class.'

Someone cleared a throat, a bit too ostentatiously. Evidently Bramwell was still in their midst. Oh well, it was up to him when he chose to rescue his mother. He must be enjoying the respite as much as any of them. More, since he wasn't being chivvied into dancing attendance on Lauren.

'Dinner is going to be late, is it?' A bit later Roberta popped her head round the corner.

'The later the better, I'd say, wouldn't you?' There would then be less of the evening to struggle through. 'No one's in any hurry, are they?'

'No,' Roberta admitted. 'Although some of them have started drifting upstairs to change. I wondered if I ought to make an announcement or something—'

'Has Bramwell gone up yet?'

'No, but he can't delay it much longer. There aren't many left in the bar now. I think Reggie's planning to close it down soon.'

'I wouldn't be surprised.' Midge glanced at her watch. 'Oh dear, it's later than I thought.'

'It's later than Bramwell realizes, too,' Roberta said. 'Amaryllis is going to be in such a screaming temper when he lets her out, he'll be lucky if she doesn't scalp him.'

'He'd better stop putting it off,' Midge said. 'No one else

is going to do it. And if she misses a meal, she'll be even more furious.'

'I'll see if I can't get him moving,' Roberta sighed. 'Maybe I ought to follow him up and bring along a good stiff drink. That might soothe her a bit.' She went back to the bar.

A familiar yowl sounded at Midge's feet and Ackroyd hurled himself against her ankles. 'What are you doing here?' she asked, startled. 'I left you in the kitchen. You know you're—'

'I'm sorry, Midge.' Dix came into the dining-room. 'I'm afraid I let him out. I heard him crying and I just opened the kitchen door an inch or so to speak to him and he pushed through and got away from me.'

'We never allow him in the dining-room.' Midge frowned at Ackroyd, since Dix was a guest. 'He knows that.'

'It's my fault entirely—'

Ackroyd, aware of Midge's displeasure, retreated from her hastily and went to sniff at Dix's shoes. He put out a paw and toyed with one of Dix's shoelaces.

'Look at that!' Dix said. 'Just like *The Third Man*. This is a brilliant cat, Midge.' He stooped and gathered Ackroyd into his arms.

'He watches the Late Film,' Midge said drily.

'All right.' Dix bowed his head. 'Perhaps I got carried away. It happens to us cat-lovers, you know. I fully understand why they worshipped them in Ancient Egypt. In fact, I have always felt an affinity for the Egyptians for that very reason. Any people smart enough to venerate the feline species—'

'That's it,' Reggie said briskly, coming into the room. 'I've closed the bar until after dinner.'

'A very wise move,' Dix said. 'Otherwise some people would never move.'

'They're moving now—' Reggie looked around. 'Need any help in here?'

'Thanks, but everything's under control—'

A sudden piercing scream sounded above them.

'That's Roberta! What on earth—' Midge led the dash for the staircase.

'Oh, what is it now?' Alice Dain asked fearfully, as they bumped into her at the head of the stairs. 'I thought the game was over.'

The screams were coming from the Barbour suite.

'I knew she'd have hysterics as soon as he let her out.' Evelina appeared in the doorway of her own suite, lipstick still in hand. 'Pity he couldn't have left her in there for the rest of the night.'

'We shouldn't have let him come up alone,' Stan said guiltily, as they crowded into the Barbour suite. 'We knew she was going to raise hell.'

'Roberta came up with him—' Midge was still in the lead as they reached the bathroom door. 'And that's her screaming.'

Bramwell was slumped against the washbasin, staring incredulously at the sight in the bathtub. Roberta was backed against the far wall, screaming mechanically, pointlessly. It was too late for screams to bring any help.

Amaryllis Barbour lay fully dressed in the tub, her eyes staring up slightlessly through the clear water. A faintly blue tinge to her pallor, a slight parboiling of her skin, told them that she had lain submerged for a very long time.

CHAPTER 21

'Jeez! Did you ever think you'd see anything like that? Just like the Brides in the Bath case.'

'Not quite—she was fully dressed.'

'Well, hell! It woulda been easier to drown her than to try to undress her.'

'And did you see the way her ankles were sticking up out of the other end of the tub? That was the way they did it, all right. Pushed her in, then gave her ankles a quick jerk and pulled her under the water. She'd have gone out like a light.'

'What do you mean *they*? *They* who?'

'Maybe . . . the Chandler *they*? They—she's crazy enough for anything.'

'I don't know . . .' Dix shook his head thoughtfully. 'Doesn't that strike you as perhaps too obvious an answer? Perhaps . . . what someone *wanted* us to think?'

'Huh? You mean—?'

'That's right. He means it's all too pat. The Chandler dame, in one personality or the other, locked Amaryllis in —and admits it. So we're supposed to think that the other one—or whichever one she thought she was at the moment —went ahead and finished the job. Talk about the left hand not knowing what the right hand is doing—'

They could still eat, Midge thought incredulously, watching them wade into the Swedish meatballs, the mounds of mashed potatoes, the green beans and cauliflower flowerets.

Of course, it was easier for them. Most of them had caught no more than a glimpse of Amaryllis in the bath before Reggie had herded them out of the Barbour suite and locked the door. To them, it was almost an extension of the game they had been playing.

They had not had to help lift the dripping body from the bath, swathe it in towels, carry it down through the narrow service passages and, finally, set it down beside Brigid's body in the outside store cupboard.

Midge felt that she might never eat again.

'I suppose it was too late for the Kiss of Life?' asked someone at another table who had missed all the excitement.

'Far too late.' Bertha wielded the gravy boat with a lavish hand, pouring the rich brown fluid over everything on her plate. 'Anyway, I'm of the generation that never did catch up with such new-fangled notions. The last time I took a First Aid Course, we were taught the old roll-'em-over-on-their-stomach technique. Then we straddled them and began the old one-two routine.'

'Artificial respiration,' Haila supplied. 'I should think that would still be more sensible for drowning cases. It would pump the water out at the same time it was pushing the air in.'

'No, thank you—' Cedric shuddered as Bertha offered him the gravy boat. 'I have enough.' He had scarcely touched his food.

'All right?' Reggie asked in passing.

'I think so.' Midge gave him a wan smile. They were the only two serving. Lettie was upstairs with a shocked and stunned Bramwell. The Barbour suite had been locked until the police could examine it and Bramwell had transferred, at her suggestion, to the spare bedroom in Evelina's suite. It would save opening up and heating another room; besides which, Bramwell was in no condition to be left alone. Unlike the remaining Chandler, he had not the capacity to absorb the missing personality into his own.

'I've said it before—' At Dix's table, the argument was still raging. 'And I'll say it again: *cui bono?*'

'I don't think she's wealthy in her own right,' Asey said. 'All the money comes from Bramwell's books. The only benefit anyone would get from her death is peace and quiet.'

'Precisely,' Dix said. 'And who needs that most?'

'Oh, now, wait a minute,' Stan protested. 'You can't mean that. Poor old Bram's all broken up about it.'

'Is he? I wonder how long he'll remain that way. He's got Lettie to comfort him, hasn't he?'

'Yeah, but how about Roberta?' Stan was going down fighting. 'She'd have a lot more peaceful life without that old bat flitting around. I happen to know she haunted Death On Wheels, always complaining that they hadn't ordered enough of Bram's books, pulling them off the shelves and trying to sneak them into the window, hiding other authors' books and generally making a damned nuisance of herself. Besides, it would have been easier for another woman to walk into the bathroom with Amaryllis there. She could have suggested Amaryllis have a nice soothing bath before

she came downstairs again. Amaryllis wouldn't think anything of her staying there talking to her while the bath filled,
maybe sitting on the edge of the tub—'

'She would have been a pushover,' Asey agreed. 'Literally.
On the other hand, Dix mentioned Lettie just now. With
his mother gone, she'd have a clear field with Bramwell—
and she's kind of sweet on him. And then, it's always possible
that it *was* the Chandler woman. We all know she's
crazy.'

They covertly observed Lauren, who was sitting between
Ned and Algie at a nearby table. At the moment, their
demeanour was more that of jailers than of suitors. It was
clear that they did not quite trust Lauren themselves. Nor
did anyone else; the table was otherwise deserted.

'I think this is awful,' Alice Dain complained as Reggie
set her dessert before her. 'When are the police going to get
here? The proper police. There must be some way we can
call them.'

'We don't have a radio transmitter, madam,' Reggie said
coldly.

'Well, there must be something we can do. Why don't we
go out and trample a message in the snow? We can stamp
out: HELP. And then any helicopters flying overhead would
see it and know we were in trouble.'

'They'd probably drop a bale of hay,' her husband said
gloomily.

'Not if we stamped out the word POLICE, too. Then
they'd know we needed them.'

'An excellent idea, madam.' Reggie forbore to ask when
she had last seen a helicopter overhead. 'We'll attend to it
first thing in the morning.'

Midge met Reggie's eyes over their heads. With any luck,
he'd be in the town by the time the guests were stirring in the
morning. Perhaps she could set some of them to trampling
messages in the snow. It would keep them occupied.

Meanwhile, there was the long evening to be got through.
The guests adjourned to the drawing-room for coffee and

liqueurs. Lingering over the port had lost its charm for the gentlemen after the first evening, perhaps because they craved something stronger, or perhaps because they were afraid of missing something. They arranged themselves around the room in small companionable groups.

'Sit beside me, Norman.' Alice clutched her husband's arm suddenly as he was about to take another seat and pulled him down beside her on the sofa, cutting out Haila, who had been about to sit there. Something in her tone made Midge look at the groupings more closely.

Were they so companionable, after all? Or were they just clinging to the people they knew best with the object of mutual protection?

The actors had volunteered to give an impromptu entertainment to while away the evening. An offer gratefully accepted. A Musical Evening was also in keeping with the Thirties theme and, perhaps not so curiously, the guests seemed determined to cling to that theme. Perhaps because they felt it distanced them from the actual murders. Some of them still seemed inclined to consider them part of the game. There was time enough for reality to burst in upon them in the morning.

'How's Bramwell?' Midge asked as Lettie came down to do her turn, a slightly bawdy Music Hall song.

'Still in a state of shock,' Lettie said. 'It's too bad he had to be the one to find her. He keeps brooding that, if he'd only gone up earlier—'

'Are you sure he didn't?' Haila had overheard. '*Some* people think maybe he did.'

'What?' For a moment, Lettie did not seem to understand, then she paled with rage. 'That's a rotten thing to insinuate! His own mother—'

'That's why.' Haila shrugged. 'You can't deny that life is going to be a lot easier for him without her around. Maybe—' Pointedly, she did not look at Lettie. 'Maybe a lot easier for other people, too, He can do what he wants now.'

Wisely, she did not wait around for Lettie's reaction, but hurriedly returned to the drawing-room.

'Is that what they're all saying?' Lettie demanded of Midge. 'Do they all believe that Bram—' She caught herself. 'Of course, they'd rather believe that than that one of themselves did it.'

'I'm sure they don't all believe it,' Midge said quickly. One or two of them were discussing that possibility, but quite a few of them favoured other candidates—' She broke off awkwardly.

'Yes,' Lettie said reflectively. 'I suppose my name *is* being bandied about.'

'Well . . . er . . .' Lettie would not be fobbed off with a lie, however well-intentioned. 'Among others.'

'That tears it!' Ned was playing Lettie's introduction; she swept off to make her entrance.

'Are we holding the line?' In the lull of business, Reggie came out from behind the bar to stand beside Midge watching the entertainers at the far end of the drawing-room.

'What line?' Midge leaned against him briefly. 'Reggie, what are we going to do? What if . . . if there's another murder?'

'Steady on.' He looked out over the audience. 'Cedric can take over the bar shortly. I'm not going to wait for daybreak, I'm going to start for town as soon as the party breaks up. Some of you can get out in the snow first thing in the morning before the guests are stirring and stamp out the suggested message. Be sure to spread out and leave lots of footprints all over the area—that ought to cover my tracks. It will be safer if no one suspects that real help may be on the way.'

'Holding the line,' Midge said bitterly. 'Oh, Reggie, I wish you didn't have to go. I . . . I'm afraid.'

There was a burst of applause as Lettie finished her song and shouts of 'Encore'. But Lettie shook her head. She crossed over to have a quiet word with Grace Holloway, then bore down on Midge and Reggie, the light of battle in her eye.

'Where are you going?' Midge asked uneasily.

'I'm going to fight!' Lettie declared. 'I've had enough. It was all very well when it was part of the game, but the game is over. They're playing with life and death now—Bramwell's life. And mine. I'm not having it!'

Miss Holloway took her place at the piano and ran a few trills before announcing: 'The actors have entertained us so splendidly during this weekend, I think it's time we returned the compliment. I happen to know that Colonel Heather does a stirring rendition of *Mandalay*—perhaps we can persuade him to oblige . . .' She led the applause as the Colonel rose and went over to stand by the piano.

'Grace is going to keep watch,' Lettie said. 'She'll signal me if anyone leaves the room.'

'What are you going to do?' Reggie asked.

'It's time for me to turn down the beds—' Lettie smiled innocently, then her smile hardened. 'I'm also going to turn over their rooms. There *must* be something to find that will give us a clue to this whole thing. There *has* to be.'

'You can't get through them all by yourself,' Reggie said. 'There are too many of them, but that's not a bad idea. I'll come along and help.'

'So will—' Midge began.

'No, you stay here. We can't all go missing. They'll suspect something.'

While Colonel Heather was looking eastward to the sea, Lettie and Reggie disappeared to begin searching the rooms. Midge perched on the arm of a chair just inside the doorway and tried to look absorbed in the entertainment and not as though she were keeping a lookout.

An air of unreality settled over her. They were all such pleasant people as, in her experience, keen mystery fans usually turned out to be. They were intelligent, friendly, literate—and one of them was deadly. But which one?

It was impossible to tell just from their appearance or demeanour.

'I can do card tricks—' Stanley Marric jumped up eagerly as the Colonel took his bow. 'If I could just have the assistance of someone in the audience. Bertha—how about you?'

'Oh, why not?' She pushed herself out of her chair and lumbered over to stand beside him resignedly.

'Great!' A pack of cards had materialized, seemingly from nowhere. 'Now, if you just take a card—any card—'

Stanley Marric? He'd claimed to be a lawyer, but he seemed occasionally to lack the polish one usually associated with lawyers. Perhaps that was why he identified with Arthur Crook. Yet why should he want to kill Brigid Chandler and Amaryllis Barbour?

Why should any of them? It kept coming back to that. Both women were undoubtedly irritating nuisances—pains in the neck, their compatriots would say—but that was scarcely sufficient reason to murder them.

Cui bono? Dix's repetition of the question was having its insidious effect. A truthful answer had to be: Bramwell Barbour and/or Lettie. It was axiomatic that most murders were domestic affairs. Was Bramwell the worm that had finally turned? Had Lettie chosen the Lady Macbeth rôle, urging him to it, acting as accomplice?

'*We* can play *Chopsticks,*' Lauren announced as Stan's card tricks ended and Bertha resumed her seat.

An embarrassed silence followed this revelation, then everyone spoke at one.

'I used to do *Casey at the Bat,*' Norman said. 'I think I can still remember it.'

'Perhaps we've had enough music for a while, dear,' Miss Holloway said hastily.

'I'll see you *Casey at the Bat* and raise you *The Boy Stood on the Burning Deck,*' Asey challenged Norman.

Midge was aware of a sudden movement in the doorway behind her. The back of her neck prickled as the hairs rose.

She turned and went limp with relief to find Reggie there.

'I didn't like leaving you alone,' Reggie said. 'Suddenly, I got nervous about it, so I came back.'

'I'm glad you did.' She sank back in her chair. 'Have you found anything?'

'Not so far. I've had a word with Dad. He's taking over my part of the search. What's going on here?'

'Amateur night, but it's keeping them amused.'

'That's the main concern.' There were footsteps on the stairs and Reggie turned quickly.

'We thought we'd come down for a while—' Evelina T. Carterslee was leading an unseeing Bramwell Barbour. 'Bramwell had some tea and toast earlier, but I'm sure he could use a drink . . . or two.'

Evelina looked as though she could use a couple herself. Was it her idea to bring Bramwell down? Or had Lettie, determined to spare no one in her efforts to clear Bramwell's name, persuaded them to leave Evelina's suite so that she could also search that?

'Sit here, Bram—' Midge rose hastily and guided Bramwell into the armchair. He didn't look as though he could walk much farther. 'All right?'

'Thank you.' He sank into the chair and looked up at her as though she could supply an explanation. 'I just don't understand it. Why should anyone want to kill Mother?'

'It was a great tragedy.' Inured by decades of purveying fiction, Evelina was able to utter the line without a visible qualm. 'But you mustn't let it crush you. Your mother would have been the last person in the world to wish to see you so upset.'

'You're right, of course.' Bramwell took a deep breath. 'I'll try to pull myself together.'

'Let me get you that drink,' Reggie said.

'Hey,' someone called, 'is the bar open?' Several of them fled the recitation as others had fled the burning deck. Reggie was caught and kept busy filling orders. Midge went and collected the drinks for Bramwell and Evelina.

'We want to play *Chopsticks*,' Lauren-Brigid pouted. 'We won a prize for it at school.'

'You can do it later, dear,' Miss Holloway said firmly. 'It's the Interval now—and the bar is open.'

The audience retreated *en masse* to the bar, giving point to her words. Midge made a mental bet that they were not going to reassemble for further entertainment without a fight. Especially if that entertainment were to include *Chopsticks*.

'It's not fair—' She was not the only one to have come to that conclusion, Haila Bond had also reached it. 'I didn't get to do my party piece—and I'm pretty damned good at it.'

'What do you do?' Alice Dain asked cautiously.

'Magic—I'm an amateur magician. And nothing like your lousy card tricks, either. Real mystifying stuff.'

'What's wrong with card tricks?' Stanley was stung. 'They're good clean fun—and they don't need a lot of equipment.'

'I don't need equipment. All it takes is just a few simple donations from the audience, things everybody carries around with them anyway. For instance, somebody let me have a lipstick—'

'Don't you have one?'

'Of course I do, Alice. That's not the point. The idea is to get the audience involved. Come on, give me your lipstick.'

'Oh, all right.' Alice rummaged in her handbag and produced a lipstick.

'Thank you. And now, I need a gentleman's handkerchief. Come on, boys, don't be shy. It won't come to any harm. How about this gentleman here—?'

She reached out and twitched Dix's handkerchief from his breast pocket. Something fell to the floor as she did so.

'Oops, sorry—' She stooped to pick it up. So did Dix.

'What's this?' Norman was swifter than either of them. He retrieved it and held it up with a puzzled expression. 'Some kind of good luck charm?'

'No—' Reggie moved out from behind the bar and snatched the small segment of wire from Norman's hand. 'I'm afraid it's just brought Dix some very bad luck. That's the piece of telephone wire the murderer cut out of our line to disable it.'

'That's the evidence we've been looking for!' Lettie cried from the doorway. 'Only the murderer could possess it. *He* killed Brigid and Amaryllis!'

CHAPTER 22

'You mean to say Dixon Carr killed my mother?' Bramwell was incredulous. 'In heaven's name, why?'

'I came here with the intention of killing you,' Dixon Carr confessed. 'However, it did not take me long to realize that *she* was the real author of most of my troubles.'

'Don't be absurd,' Bramwell said. 'How could she be? We've never seen you before in our lives.'

'Aha—of course you'd never seen me. You hadn't the decency to confront me in person. Instead, you set your lawyers on me to persecute me, to hound me out of my living, to ruin my life.'

'What's he talking about?' Stanley Marric wanted to know. 'No lawyers could do all that to him. Not unless he'd been guilty of something pretty spectacular in the first place.'

'I was guilty of nothing! I was an innocent man, innocently engaged in my lawful occupation. I was ... *The Sphinx!*'

'The—what?' Bramwell said.

'Is he trying to cop an insanity plea?' Stan asked.

'Wait a minute—wait a minute,' Bertha said. 'I've got it!

The Sphinx was that critic everybody kept suing. They finally ran him out of town.'

'Good God!' Bramwell said. 'Was that you?'

'The same.' Dix bowed gravely. 'You will agree, Mr Barbour, that I have had every right to carry a grudge against you.'

'Maybe so,' Algie said. 'But why did you kill Brigid?'

'Aha—because *Bramwell* had every good reason to want her out of the way. Actually, it needn't have been her—either one of them would have done.'

Midge looked around nervously and was in time to see Algie and Roberta quietly removing Lauren from the room before she could realize what was being revealed.

'You were trying to get Bramwell blamed for the murders!' Lettie accused. 'And that was why you killed his mother, too. So that everyone would think he'd done it.'

'Not the sole reason.' Dix allowed himself a quiet smile. 'After I had seen the . . . lady . . . in action, it was a pleasure to dispose of her. I knew then that she alone must have been the moving spirit behind the lawsuit that lost me my position on the newspaper. Bramwell would never have bothered, if it were left to him.

'I was able to slip up the service stairs after we discovered that she had been locked in the bathroom and no one was going to exert themselves to rescue her in a hurry. She thought I'd come to let her out. I had the satisfaction of revealing my true identity before I knocked her unconscious. I then filled the tub with water and submerged her. It was very apt, I thought. They always drowned witches in the old days. And the beauty of it was that Bramwell was certain to be Suspect Number One.'

'I can't believe this—' Cedric shook his head groggily. 'Do you mean to tell us that you killed two people so that a third person would be blamed for it? That's impossible. People don't *do* things like that.'

'On the contrary,' Bertha said, 'they did them all the time in the Golden Age. It was a favourite plot. That, and the series murders, when several innocent bystanders were killed just to obscure the fact that one of the victims was intended. That was another drawback about the Golden Age: it was awfully hard on innocent bystanders.'

'I've read them all.' Dix sighed reminiscently. 'There were no books like them. They don't write them like that any more.'

'They'd never get away with it, these days,' Evelina said.

'I'm proud to say—' Dix eyed her coldly; it was probably as well for her that his activities were now curtailed—'I'm *very* proud to say that I haven't read a book dated later than 1940 since I stopped reviewing. Not in the past fifteen years.'

'I'm sorry to say,' Evelina murmured bitterly, 'there are too many people like you around.'

'You overdosed on those old books,' Bertha said. 'They went to your head. Of course, that was how you knew about the service stairs. You'd absorbed so many country house backgrounds you knew servants' passages would have to exist in a place like Chortlesby Manor.'

'Precisely. Poor Brigid was quite thrilled when I offered to share my secret staircase with her.' He sighed. 'It was rather a pity, I had nothing personal against the girl, despite her irritating personality.'

'Brigid . . . Mother . . .' Bramwell was stunned. Lettie put her arms around him consolingly. 'Was it going to be me next?'

'Certainly not.' Dix seemed annoyed at his obtuseness. 'Haven't you been paying attention? You were going to take the rap, as they say. Swing for those murders—or, at least, spend a great many years in prison . . .'

'Well, hell . . .' Stan said into the sudden silence. 'What do we do now?'

What indeed? They looked at each other uneasily. Dix stood there unconcerned; he seemed to be preoccupied with some private thoughts.

'You're under arrest, Mr Carr,' Reggie said. 'You do know that, don't you?'

'Oh yes, yes.' He shrugged it off as a matter of no importance. 'That's quite in keeping.' He smiled to himself.

Several people standing near him moved back uneasily.

'Suppose you can't ask the fellow for his parole,' Colonel Heather said. 'Too *non compos* for that.'

'Aha—Colonel Primrose!' Dix winked at him.

Colonel Heather moved back uneasily.

'I'm going to strike out for town,' Reggie said. 'If I can make it to the highway, it should have been ploughed by now and perhaps I can flag down a ride. I'll bring the police back with me. Meanwhile, we'll have to lock him in his room.'

'Mount a guard over the door,' Colonel Heather advised. 'I'll take the first watch myself.'

'Good idea.' Reggie took Dix's arm. 'If you'll just come along—'

'—quietly, I know.' Docilely, Dix allowed himself to be led out into the lobby, towards the staircase.

He was taking it so quietly that they all began to relax. It was not until he reached the foot of the stairs that he suddenly broke free of Reggie, hurled him back against those immediately behind them, and raced down the corridor towards the kitchen.

'After him!'

'Don't let him get away!'

Amidst much shouting, they disentangled themselves. There were answering shouts and shrieks from the kitchen.

Suddenly the entire Manor was plunged into blackness.

'The lights!' Reggie swore briefly and luridly. 'The bugger's done for the lights.'

'We should have expected something like this.' Bertha spoke with calm reasonableness. 'I remember reading somewhere that The Sphinx wound up working for an electricity company. He'd have learned all about things like that. I wouldn't count on getting the electricity working again until morning.'

'Midge—candles!' Reggie shouted.

'Yes. Oh, sorry . . . Excuse me . . . Sorry . . .' Midge bumped into one after another as she made her way to the bar where they had a small emergency supply. Everyone was milling about. Dix could be back in their midst and they'd never know it. The thought was frightening.

'What's going on?' Roberta called from the top of the stairs. 'What's the matter?'

'He's gone! He got away!' Shouts from several throats enlightened her.

'Oh, really?' The information did not appear to disturb her unduly. She could be heard beginning a cautious descent.

'What's happened?' A tiny flame wavered towards them down the kitchen corridor. 'Who was that maniac who rushed through my kitchen?' Cook hovered between tears and fury. 'What has he done with Mr Eric?'

'Eric?' Midge began lighting candles and passing them to those nearest her. 'What do you mean?'

'That madman grabbed him. It was the last thing I saw before the lights went out.'

'My God—Dad!' Reggie grabbed a candle and raced for the kitchen at such speed that it nearly blew out. He had to stop and shield it with one hand before proceeding. The others crowded after him.

'Dad!' Reggie shouted. 'Dad—where are you?'

Two faint complaining cries answered him. Reggie ignored the one from Ackroyd.

'Dad—where are you?'

'Here.' Eric came reeling into view from the private wing. Reggie rushed to him.

'Dad—are you all right?'

'No. No, I'm not. I've just been mugged! Mugged—in my own home!'

'Here, take it easy, Dad. Sit down.' Reggie pulled out a chair for him.

'The cooking brandy!' Cook rushed to get it. Eric groaned.

'Did he hurt you, Dad? Where did he go?'

'He grabbed me and hustled me to my room,' Eric complained. 'He's gone off with my passport, my topcoat and my wallet. He said he'd send everything back to me from Ceylon. I don't believe him for a minute.'

'Ceylon! Jeez—he *is* crazy.'

'I'm going after him—' Reggie started for the door.

'Oh no you're not!' Midge grabbed him and held on tight. Norman and Asey moved forward to reinforce her.

'No point in that, Reggie,' Asey said. 'He won't get far. Especially if he's trying to buy a ticket for Ceylon.'

'Let the police worry about him,' Norman advised. 'They'll catch him fast enough, if he's running around acting like it's 1935.'

'But the police don't even know what's happened yet. I'll have to tell them—'

'Morning is time enough now,' Roberta said calmly. 'The police aren't going to hold you responsible for not notifying them when we've been cut off like this. And, as Norman says, they'll soon catch him.'

'It'll be an insanity plea, for sure,' Stan decided. 'I may take the case myself.'

It was a very satisfactory conclusion for Roberta, Midge realized. There would now be no reason to delay the tour's departure. The police had a self-confessed murderer to hunt. Perhaps it was even a satisfactory conclusion for *Murder At The Manor*. Even without the American tours, the resultant publicity would ensure a rush of bookings to carry them through the next couple of seasons. Midge suddenly felt more cheerful.

'But—' Reggie continued to struggle. Midge looked around for additional help and saw Bertha raise her foot and aim it at Eric's shin. In the dim candlelight, the move went unnoticed by the others.

'Aaargh!' Eric bellowed.

'Dad!' Reggie whirled, this time they let him go. He rushed to Eric's side. 'You *are* hurt!'

'My leg—I think it's broken,' Eric groaned.

'Here—let me see. You shouldn't have been walking on it—'

'That's right,' Bertha approved. 'You worry about your Dad and never mind chasing maniacs through the snow. I could help you rig up a splint.'

'Here we are—' Cook emerged from the cellar juggling three large dusty bottles. 'We've all had a nasty shock. A nice drop of the cooking brandy is what we need.'

'Don't drop them!' Eric cried. 'In fact, don't even open them!'

'Don't be silly, Mr Eric—' The guests were already clustering around Cook; even Ackroyd had joined the hopeful throng. 'It will do us all a world of good.'

Eric groaned.